"I want to be inside you, Matty," Sebastian pleaded

He didn't care that he sounded desperate. He was desperate. "Please get the—"

"Yes," Matty murmured, taking a condom from the drawer.

"Now, Matty," he said hoarsely, battling for control as she put the condom on. Then the mattress shifted and she rested her hands on his shoulders. He opened his eyes and looked up into hers. Bracketing her waist with both hands, he held her gaze as he guided her down. Her eyes were luminous. He knew he'd never forget the way they looked at this moment.

Easy. Slow. There. He drew in a sharp breath. So good. He couldn't imagine it getting any better than this. "Ride me, Matty," he whispered urgently.

Lips parted, eyes bright, she did just that, giving him the trip of his life. There was no holding back. Stunned by the impact, he couldn't hear anything beyond the pounding of his heart. Then a high-pitched noise penetrated the haze surrounding him.
His baby.

D1012720

woman. Very pretty.

Dear Reader,

As much as I adore cowboys, I also love torturing the sexy rascals. In my new miniseries, THREE COWBOYS & A BABY, each of them thinks he's the father of the same darling baby girl, which makes for some very tense moments. Cowboys. They're so cute when they're angry.

First up is Sebastian Daniels. Sebastian has a tough time adjusting to the idea that the bundle of joy left on his doorstep might be *his* bundle of joy. But once he latches on to the concept, he won't be denied. Unfortunately for him, his good buddy Travis Evans stakes a claim to the baby in *Two in the Saddle,* available in May. In *Boone's Bounty,* a June release, Sebastian's loyal friend Boone Connor insists the little girl definitely belongs to him. Three men. One baby. Could it get any more complicated?

Yes. Because there's a fourth cowboy—Nat Grady. For the thrilling conclusion of this miniseries, I'm stepping out of Temptation and into the realm of Single Titles. Don't miss *That's My Baby!* in September.

Warmly,

Vicki Lewis Thompson

Vicki Lewis Thompson
THE COLORADO KID

HARLEQUIN®

TORONTO • NEW YORK • LONDON
AMSTERDAM • PARIS • SYDNEY • HAMBURG
STOCKHOLM • ATHENS • TOKYO • MILAN • MADRID
PRAGUE • WARSAW • BUDAPEST • AUCKLAND

If you purchased this book without a cover you should be aware
that this book is stolen property. It was reported as "unsold and
destroyed" to the publisher, and neither the author nor the
publisher has received any payment for this "stripped book."

To Roz Denny Fox,
for her unselfish support and friendship.
Thanks, Roz.

ISBN 0-373-25880-1

THE COLORADO KID

Copyright © 2000 by Vicki Lewis Thompson.

All rights reserved. Except for use in any review, the reproduction or
utilization of this work in whole or in part in any form by any electronic,
mechanical or other means, now known or hereafter invented, including
xerography, photocopying and recording, or in any information storage
or retrieval system, is forbidden without the written permission of the
publisher, Harlequin Enterprises Limited, 225 Duncan Mill Road,
Don Mills, Ontario, Canada M3B 3K9.

All characters in this book have no existence outside the imagination of
the author and have no relation whatsoever to anyone bearing the same
name or names. They are not even distantly inspired by any individual
known or unknown to the author, and all incidents are pure invention.

This edition published by arrangement with Harlequin Books S.A.

® and TM are trademarks of the publisher. Trademarks indicated with
® are registered in the United States Patent and Trademark Office, the
Canadian Trade Marks Office and in other countries.

Visit us at www.eHarlequin.com

Printed in U.S.A.

1

"COME ON, SEBASTIAN, HONEY." Charlotte eased back from his kiss and reached for the zipper of his fly. "Show little ol' Charlotte what's inside those Wranglers."

Sebastian grabbed her hand and moved it aside. Damned if he liked having a woman set the pace. Besides, it'd been a long time, and he couldn't have her fumbling around when he wasn't sure how good his control would be. "We'll get to that," he muttered.

"How sweet." She nibbled at his bottom lip as she flicked open a snap on his western shirt. "You're shy. I never would've guessed you'd be shy after being married to Barbara." She popped another snap open. "Is that why you cooked me that special dinner, served us wine and built a fire in the fireplace, so you'd get over being nervous?"

His jaw clenched. "I'm not nervous. I just like to—"

"Me, too, honey." She ripped the rest of the buttons open and plunged her tongue halfway down his throat.

Hell, he was getting worked up, and he'd just figured out he didn't like Charlotte all that much. He believed you should at least like a woman you intended to take to bed. He'd liked her okay every time he'd seen her behind her desk at Colorado Savings and Loan. And spring was coming on, the season of the year he always felt the most like planting...something. In another month he'd be thirty-five years old and he could feel time passing. But maybe inviting Charlotte out to the ranch had been a bad idea.

She moaned and shoved her D-cups against his chest. "Undress me," she whispered before delving into his mouth again. The woman had a tongue like a backhoe. But those D-cups did tempt him. They were two of the items that had caught his interest in the first place. And as his friends had been telling him, he had to start somewhere if he expected to get back in the hunt.

Still, if it'd been left up to him, he probably wouldn't have moved the evening along quite this fast. It didn't seem to be up to him, however, and if he didn't do something manly soon she'd be insulted. He unfastened the delicate top button of her blouse, pleased that he hadn't lost the technique.

With the way her chest was heaving, he needed all the technique he could remember to unbutton her blouse and unfasten the front latch on her bra. He'd had easier times taking the bucking strap off a bronc. But at last he had clear access, and he had to admit she filled a man's hands to overflowing. Too bad her perfume nearly made him choke.

But he could deal with that. Would deal with that. Because now his jeans were uncomfortably tight, and Charlotte seemed only too eager to help him with his problem. Besides, he'd invited her out to join him for dinner with this sort of activity in the back of his mind. He'd even made Fleafarm bed down in the barn so the dog wouldn't be underfoot.

He'd served dinner by candlelight, and afterward, when she'd suggested they leave the lights off and sit by the fire for a while with their wine, he'd made no objection. She could rightly accuse him of being a tease if he didn't follow through. Maybe he'd discover he liked her better as they went along. And he had to start somewhere.

JESSICA FELT as if she'd driven over half the state of Colorado trying to make sure nobody had followed her jam-packed Subaru out of Aspen. Or maybe she'd been putting off the moment that had to come.

It was close now. She'd picked up a cup of coffee at a convenience mart in Canon City. Then she'd pushed on to the little town of Huerfano. A few miles beyond Huerfano the pavement ended, signaling that she was nearly there.

Sebastian had asked her to visit the Rocking D a hundred times, but she'd never found the time. Then she'd become pregnant and a visit would have raised questions she'd rather not answer yet. Now the Rocking D and Sebastian were her best hope for protecting Elizabeth, her sweet innocent child sleeping in a padded car seat amidst a jumble of belongings.

Jessica thought briefly of her parents, secure in their walled and gated estate on the Hudson River. Elizabeth would be protected there, as Jessica had been protected for the first twenty-four years of her life, although she wouldn't truly call it a life. She wouldn't wish that kind of stifling existence on anyone, let alone her own daughter.

When she left home three years ago, she'd felt confident she could blend into the woodwork and become an ordinary citizen as long as she had minimal contact with her parents and kept a low profile. But apparently someone had found out she was the Franklin heir. She'd had enough kidnapping escape drills as a kid to recognize that somebody had tried to snatch her. Because they'd tried to snatch her after work when Elizabeth was home with a nanny, Jessica figured they must not know about the baby. And she wanted it to stay that way.

For the past few days she'd put blinders on her emotions, focusing on the next steps, trying to turn the nightmare into the sort of interesting science experiment that would have challenged her in college. She'd bought several wigs to cover her red hair then traded her royal blue car in for the nondescript gray Subaru. Mechanically she'd packed, leaving in the middle of the night hoping that no one would see her. And for three days, she'd been gradually switching Elizabeth to formula.

The moon picked out fragments of ice in the dirt road, making them glitter like broken glass. Patches of snow gleamed in open areas between stands of juniper. Thank God the weather was still cold enough that the road was frozen instead of muddy. Getting stuck out here would be disastrous.

And thank God Sebastian was home tonight. She'd called earlier from Canon City, pretending to be a carpet-cleaning service when he'd answered. His strong, gentle voice, sounding slightly impatient over the unwanted sales call but still kind, had brought tears to her eyes. He was such a good friend. How she longed to pour out the whole horrible story and run to him for comfort and advice. But she couldn't risk it.

She drove slowly, searching the road on her right for the ranch entrance. When it rose up out of the darkness—two sturdy poles braced by a third across the top—a dagger of pain sliced past her defenses and left her gasping. She stopped the car and gripped the wheel until she was in control of herself again.

Behind her, Elizabeth whimpered softly in her sleep.

The soft, vulnerable sound nearly destroyed her, but it was the one sound she needed to hear. Swallowing a sob of anguish, she turned down the road leading to the ranch.

SEBASTIAN WANTED to move the whole program from the leather sofa, where Charlotte was lying half-naked, to the bedroom, where he'd have space to stretch his legs during the proceedings and the surface wouldn't be so damned slippery. Besides, he'd stashed a couple of condoms in the drawer of his bedside table, figuring that was the logical place for them if and when they needed to be deployed. He hadn't counted on Charlotte seducing him in the living room.

Now she seemed too involved to welcome a change of scenery, and he didn't think he could carry her without risk of damage to both of them.

He levered himself away from her. "Charlotte, I need—"

"You need me, honey!" She grabbed his belt buckle and pulled him back down.

"Yeah, but first I have to get—"

"Undressed." She had his buckle open in record

time. She must have worked on belt buckles a time or two before this.

"Birth control," he said around her eager kisses. He was off-balance and couldn't stop her from tugging down his zipper without falling flat onto her.

"I have that covered." She reached inside his jeans. "Don't you worry about a thing."

He closed his eyes and tried to tell himself that he trusted her to take care of that detail. But he didn't. With a groan he pulled away from her again. "I'm getting the condoms."

"I'll have you know I have no communicable diseases!" She grabbed his arm as he struggled off the sofa.

"Maybe I do," he said.

"Ha." She redoubled her efforts to pull him back to her. "You've lived like a monk since Barbara left."

"Says who?" He wrestled his way out of her arms.

"Everybody in Fremont County, that's who." Panting, she gazed up at him. "Come on, now. It'll feel *so* good without one of those little raincoats on."

It would. It most certainly would. But as much as he relished the idea, he wouldn't let himself succumb. "I don't believe in taking chances," he said.

And he never had, not in that way. He'd risked his neck a million times, but when it came to making babies, he was old-fashioned enough to believe that the father of the baby should be married to the mother. With luck they'd also be madly in love.

Charlotte gazed at him, her eyes hot. "Better hurry then, sugar. My motor's running." She glanced at his erection. "And I do believe the gearshift works."

He couldn't help smiling. Maybe this would be fun, after all, although the frantic pace didn't suit him. "Guess it does." He eased his zipper back up so his pants wouldn't fall down as he started into the bedroom. "I'll be right—"

The doorbell chimed.

He turned, hardly believing he'd heard the sound. This time of year he was alone on the ranch. Folks didn't just drop by unannounced at nine-thirty on a Friday night unless something was wrong.

Immediately he thought of his neighbor Matty. Oh, God. What if something had happened over at the Leaning L? Matty lived alone, too, a fact that often worried him. He couldn't say that to Matty, though. A more fiercely independent woman he'd never known.

He turned to Charlotte, who looked extremely put out with the interruption. He shrugged in apology. "Listen, could you go into the bedroom while I see who this is? It could be an emergency or something."

"Damn well better be an emergency," Charlotte muttered as she gathered her blouse together and climbed from the sofa. "Oh, well. I'll go make myself comfortable in your beddie-bye."

Sebastian snapped his shirt buttons and tucked the tails into his jeans. Then he buckled his belt. He hoped Matty wasn't at the door, what with Charlotte lying naked in his bed. If Matty found out, she probably wouldn't mind. She'd probably laugh about it. But it would embarrass the hell out of him.

Checking to make sure Charlotte was safely out of sight in the bedroom, he walked through semi-darkness to the front door. He'd pulled the drapes across the windows facing the porch, both for privacy and to keep the heat in on this cold March night.

When he opened the front door, he was nearly

blinded by high beams trained right on the porch. Clouds of exhaust from the vehicle billowed in the cold night air. He threw up an arm, trying to shade his eyes. "Who's there?"

The idiot driver laid on the horn.

"Hey!" He started out the door. If this was somebody's idea of a joke, he didn't appreciate it. "What the hell are you—"

He stopped abruptly as he heard a wail. A baby's wail.

Right by his feet.

He looked down and damned if there wasn't one of those baby carriers by the door. And damned if the wailing wasn't coming from a real live kid!

As he stood there, too stunned to react, the headlight beams shifted, arcing across the porch as the driver swung the vehicle around.

Sebastian charged down the porch steps. "Hold on! You can't leave a baby here like some stray dog! Come back, damn your hide! How'm I supposed to know what to do with a damned baby?" He ran a fruitless few yards, memorizing the license plate before he gave up and headed back to the porch, where the baby was still crying.

He let loose a string of oaths, his breath frosting the air as he stomped up the steps. If this didn't take the cake. Sure, he'd had the usual puppies and kittens dropped at his place. City folks seemed to think a ranch was like the local Humane Society, the perfect place to leave unwanted pets. But a baby! He couldn't get his mind around the concept.

At least he had noted the license plate of the car. Not that anyone who would do such a thing deserved to have the kid back. He'd like to see them prosecuted, though, and that was reason enough to see they were tracked down. For the time being, he'd better get this little bundle into the house where it was warm.

He started to reach for the infant seat, and in the soft glow of the porch light noticed a note was pinned to the baby's blanket.

"Sebastian?" Charlotte, barefoot and wearing only his bathrobe, approached the open front door. "Do I hear a baby out there?"

Sebastian picked up the red-faced, crying infant in its carrier and walked into the house. "Somebody dropped it off," he said, disbelief lacing his words. "Just drove up here, unloaded the kid and took off."

Charlotte backed up, a wary look on her face. "Why would they do a thing like that?"

"How should I know?" He shoved the door closed with one booted foot and switched on the overhead light by the front door with his elbow. "There's a note."

"I hate crying babies," Charlotte said.

"You'd cry, too, if somebody just left you on the porch." Sebastian leaned closer to read the slip of paper and his breath caught. This was no random drop-off. The note was specifically addressed to him. His gaze cut to the signature. *Jessica.* He hadn't seen her in months, not since his birthday last year. *Eleven months ago.* His heart rate skyrocketed and cold sweat trickled down his spine. He peered at the little red face, but he was no judge of how old a baby was.

"What does the note say?" Charlotte asked.

Sebastian was afraid to read it. God, he'd been drunk that night. They'd all been drunker than skunks—him, Travis and Boone. But not Jessica.

She'd good-naturedly driven them back to their rented cabin near the ski lodge, given them all vitamins to ward off a hangover and pushed them toward their individual beds. They'd flirted with her outrageously. He remembered pulling her down to the bed as she tucked him in, teasing her for a kiss....

"Sebastian, you're driving me nuts! What does the blasted note say?"

With the baby still crying, he forced himself to read it.

Dear Sebastian,
I'm counting on you to be a godfather to my little Elizabeth until I can return for her. Your generosity and kindness are exactly what she needs right now. Believe me, dear friend, I wouldn't do this if I weren't in desperate circumstances. Please don't contact the authorities. It's best if no one knows where Elizabeth is.
In deepest gratitude,
                                        Jessica

A godfather. She didn't say he was the father, only that she wanted him to be a godfather to this little baby. Maybe this kid was older than she looked. But the fact remained that Jessica was in trouble, and she'd delivered her baby to his doorstep. That was pretty damned incriminating.

"Well?" Charlotte's impatience was obvious.

He glanced at her. "Know anything about babies?"

She held up a hand and backed up a couple more steps. "Not a thing, sugar, except how you make one." She tilted her head toward the wailing child. "Did you make this one?"

"I don't know. I don't remember."

"Oh, yeah, that's what they all say. Funny how amnesia strikes when a guy faces a moment like this."

That did it. He *really* didn't like Charlotte. "Well, whether I am or not, I have to make her stop crying." He carried the infant seat over to the sofa and set it down.

"Her?"

"Her name's Elizabeth." He worked at the straps holding the baby in and finally got them undone. Then he paused, realizing that didn't solve anything because he didn't know what to do next. He should probably pick her up, but he was afraid to. She was so small, and so red in the face. He leaned toward her. "Don't cry, Elizabeth, honey. Don't cry, okay?"

Elizabeth didn't seem to understand. She opened her mouth wide and cried louder. Nothing wrong with her lungs, at least.

"I'm getting dressed and skedaddling out of here." Charlotte headed toward the bedroom. "I can't take this."

"Wait!" Panic rose in him. "You can't leave me alone with her!"

Charlotte turned back to him. "Look, I'm no good with babies. Never wanted any and never learned what to do with them. I suggest you call somebody who knows what they're doing. Or drive her in to see Doc Harrison in Huerfano."

"I can't—" He started to say he couldn't tell anybody about the baby yet, until he'd figured out if he was the father. But that was ridiculous. He had to find someone to help him take care of her, and fast. "Look, you're a woman. You must be better at this than me. At least show me how to pick her up. I've never held a kid this young."

"That makes two of us, bud. You'd better call somebody. I'm getting dressed." With that she whirled and went into the bedroom.

About the only bright spot Sebastian could see in the situation was that he hadn't made love to Charlotte, a woman he really, really didn't like. Otherwise, he couldn't remember being this confused, clumsy and uncertain in his life, except maybe the time he faced the row of girls lined up on the far side of the gym at the eighth-grade social. He didn't think he should even touch this baby without washing his hands first. He might be carrying some deadly germ.

So he patted her where the blanket covered her up, but his pats seemed to have no effect. She was getting *very* red in the face. He couldn't see her eyes because they were squeezed shut. Her head was covered with some knit thing that reminded him of the cover on a golf club, and her hands, the tiniest hands he'd ever seen in his life, were clenched and waving in the air.

Charlotte reappeared, tugging on her wool coat. As she buttoned it, she gazed at him and shook her head. Finally she sighed and stomped into the kitchen.

Hope surged through him. She was going to get something, do something, work some feminine magic to make this crying stop. Her instincts had finally kicked in, providing her with the mothering abilities that all woman carried in their genes. Maybe he'd been wrong to judge her so harshly.

She reappeared and thrust the cordless phone at him. "Here. Call somebody." Then she grabbed her purse and went out the front door, closing it firmly behind her.

Sebastian stared at the phone and finally punched in the one number he knew by heart.

FIVE YEARS AGO Matty Lang had thought of herself as a young widow. Twenty-seven wasn't old. Friends and family had assured her she'd find a good man, have kids, continue along life's path in a normal progression. Matty loved normal progressions, which was why she felt so much satisfaction sitting at her floor loom watching the design grow. Usually.

But not on a Friday night, when she knew damn well that Charlotte Crabtree from the bank was up at the Rocking D having dinner alone with Sebastian, while Matty, now thirty-two and no longer feeling so frigging *young* anymore, sat throwing a shuttle back and forth and swearing under her breath.

Sebastian would never think to invite her to dinner. Oh, no. Not good old Matty, who could ride as well as he could, and rope nearly as well. Matty sometimes wondered if he even remembered she was a woman. She, on the other hand, had never managed to forget he was a man. She'd been trying ever since the day she'd met Sebastian Daniels, the day she and Butch had moved to the Leaning L and had been welcomed by their closest neighbors Barbara and Sebastian, owners of the Rocking D.

She remembered thinking that a young bride had no business looking at another man the way she found herself looking at Sebastian. And for years she'd forced herself to ignore his considerable sex appeal—mostly. Then Butch had died, and once she'd worked through her grief, ignoring Sebastian became even tougher, especially when she could tell he and Barbara weren't getting along. After Barbara left, Matty had allowed herself to begin daydreaming, just a little.

Fat lot of good that had done her. Two years after his divorce, Sebastian still treated her exactly the way he always had, like one of the boys. Matty threw the shuttle impatiently as a picture of Charlotte Crabtree wiggled through her mind. Charlotte would never be mistaken for one of the boys.

Oh, how Charlotte had loved bragging to anyone within hearing distance about her big date with Sebastian. Matty had been so sick of listening to Charlotte this afternoon that she'd almost left without making her deposit.

Matty knew Sebastian would serve his own personal specialty—coq au vin. He used to make it for the four of them when Barbara and Butch were still around. He'd probably built a fire in the fireplace and lit some candles. Matty ground her teeth. And wine. Sebastian liked a good wine with dinner. They'd be finished by now, though, and then—what might happen after dinner didn't bear thinking about. So she wouldn't.

But she did think about it. Maybe she'd have to switch banks. It would be worth it to drive all the way into Canon City just so she didn't have to lay eyes on Charlotte Crabtree and her smug smile. Yes, that was what she'd do. She'd move her account to Canon City on Monday and find a bank that was offering free stuff for opening an account. Maybe she could get herself a new toaster oven or a set of dishes out of the deal. Or one of those bitty color television sets. She'd always wanted—

The ringing phone made her jump and she knocked over her bench. It landed with a clatter on the hardwood floor, startling Sadie, her Great Dane, out of her snooze near the loom. Nobody called at this hour on a Friday night unless it was an emergency. Heart pounding, Matty hurried into the kitchen. As she picked up the phone, she prayed it was a prank or a wrong number, and not some family disaster.

"Matty?" Sebastian sounded frantic.

Matty frowned. Unless she was mistaken, that was a baby crying in the background. She couldn't put that together with Charlotte Crabtree and the dinner date, but yes, there was definitely a very young baby close to the phone. "What's going on?"

"It's...complicated. Can you come over?"

Not while Charlotte was still there, she wouldn't. "Why?"

"Because I need you to help me."

"With what?"

"I'll explain when you get here. Please, Matty. Come quick."

"Is Charlotte still there?"

"How did you know about Charlotte?"

"Sebastian, everybody with an account at Colorado Savings knows Charlotte came up to your place for dinner. Is she still there?"

"No. Can you come over?"

So Charlotte had left and a tiny baby was there instead. Matty was burning up with curiosity. Wild horses couldn't have kept her off the Rocking D tonight. "I'll be right there," she said.

2

NO UNFAMILIAR VEHICLES sat in the circular drive in front of Sebastian's place, but Matty noticed two large cardboard boxes next to the front door when she climbed the steps to his porch. And sure enough, a baby was crying inside the house. As near as she could remember, there had never been a baby at the Rocking D, even though folks around here thought the ranch's brand looked a lot like a cradle.

She pounded on the front door, figuring she'd better make a lot of racket to be heard above the screaming baby.

The door opened almost immediately and Sebastian stood there looking frazzled. It was a novel sight. Matty couldn't remember seeing him frazzled before. The notion that he even *could* get frazzled pleased her immensely.

He'd always been in charge of himself, his feet planted firmly on the ground, his broad shoulders ready to take any weight, his gray gaze steady and sure. Over the years, his self-reliance had both thrilled and maddened her. She found that sort of confidence sexy, but it didn't leave much room for a woman to feel needed.

But tonight, he definitely needed someone, and she happened to be handy.

"Thank God you're here." He stepped back from the door. "You must have driven like a snail."

"Actually, I broke the speed limit." She imagined even five minutes would be an eternity with that caterwauling going on. She walked into the house, shucking her jacket as she went. "Where's the kid?"

"Over there." He gestured toward the sofa in front of the fire, where an infant seat held a squirming and very loud baby.

Matty had a thousand and one questions revolving around the sudden arrival of this baby at Sebastian's house on a Friday night, but she decided there was no point in asking even one of them until they got the noise level down a bit. "What have you done for it?"

"Nothing. It's a she. Elizabeth."

"Nothing?" Matty crossed to the sofa, where the baby had tangled her blanket around herself as she flailed her little arms and legs. She had on some sort of one-piece pink suit and a pink hat, which was nearly off, plus the blanket. She looked hot.

"I was afraid I'd do the wrong thing," he said. "I don't know anything about babies. So I built up the fire."

"I can see that." The heat danced off Matty's flannel shirt and jeans. She tried to ignore the pair of wineglasses on the coffee table and the distinct odor of Charlotte's perfume that still stunk up the place. In between the baby ruckus came the soft sounds of some easy-listening country music on the CD player. Sebastian had fixed himself quite a little seduction pit.

"Where's Charlotte?"

"Gone. She doesn't know anything about babies."

Well, that was something. The baby had driven Charlotte away. "I don't know much, either," Matty said. "But I think we should get her out of those clothes or away from the fire."

"You pick her up, then, okay?"

Matty glanced at him and held back a smile. Finally, *finally* she'd found something that scared the hell out of big bad Sebastian Daniels. "Okay." She hadn't handled many babies, but she seemed to remember when they were this young you got one hand under their bottom and the other one under their head, because they were still sort of floppy.

This one was pretty rigid, though, probably from crying herself into a complete frenzy. Feeling awkward, Matty scooped her up and cradled her in her arms, rocking her gently. It felt like holding a noisy five-pound sack of potatoes. Matty didn't know if her technique was any good, but the hysterical pitch of the cries softened, although the steady crying didn't stop.

Matty carried the baby away from the fire. "Settle down, Elizabeth," she instructed the baby. "Everything's okay. No need to get worked up." Matty had no idea if everything was okay or not, but the kid couldn't understand her, anyway. She sat in the old maple rocker that had been around the Rocking D for as long as Matty could remember. Holding the baby in her lap, she took off the knit cap and began unzipping the fleece suit.

"What should I do?" Sebastian asked.

"She might be hungry."

"Don't look at me!"

Matty glanced up. "There's no one else here to look at. Whose baby is this?"

He ran his fingers through his hair. "Um...we can discuss that later, after we get her settled down."

Interesting answer. She noticed his hair was a tousled mess. Either he'd been shoving his fingers into it a lot, or someone else had. Matty didn't want to think about that possibility, although she could understand the temptation. Sebastian had the kind of thick, dark brown hair that made women dream of burying their fingers in it.

"I don't know how we're going to get her settled down if you're not prepared to feed her," she said. "Did her mother leave you some formula or something?"

He looked stunned. "God, you would think she would have, and diapers and clothes, and *stuff!* Babies need stuff."

"Sebastian, you're going to have to tell me before my curiosity kills me dead. How in hell did you end up with this kid tonight?"

"She was left on the porch."

Matty's hands stilled and she stared at him. "You're kidding."

"No."

"I thought that sort of thing only happened in books." She was fascinated that Sebastian wouldn't look her in the eye. He was usually a look-you-in-the-eye sort of guy. An up-front person. And then she figured out why he might be evading her gaze, and her stomach clutched. "Is she yours?" She prayed he'd say no.

He ran his fingers through his hair again. "It's...possible."

God, it hurt. She'd imagined all this time that she knew what was going on with him. If he hadn't turned to her after Barbara left, she'd drawn comfort from the belief that he hadn't turned to anyone else, either. His date with Charlotte tonight had been tough to accept, but at least she'd known it was a first date, and she'd secretly hoped it would be a disaster.

Now she had to face the fact that he'd had a relationship with someone months ago and might have fathered a child with her. Sebastian had always wanted kids. Matty knew that had been a bone of contention in his marriage to Barbara. Matty had wanted kids, too.

Once upon a time she'd dreamed...but Sebastian didn't think of her that way, obviously. He'd found what he needed somewhere else.

She swallowed the bitter taste in her mouth, but her words came out with a sharp edge. "So who's the mother and why isn't she here?"

"She's the woman who was with us during the avalanche two years ago in Aspen, and I don't know why she's not here. Apparently she's in some kind of trouble and had to park Elizabeth for a while."

Matty remembered the ski trip on Sebastian's birthday, right after the divorce had become final. Matty had been prepared to help him celebrate both events, but Travis, Boone and Nat had lured him off for a stag weekend. When she'd seen the televised news of the avalanche, she'd fought hysteria until she'd finally learned no one had been hurt.

Then last year the guys had gone back to Aspen on his birthday again. Matty had thought they were all trying to prove they weren't afraid of some big old avalanche, but maybe Sebastian had simply wanted to celebrate his birthday with this woman. Really celebrate. "Did you know about the baby?"

He looked at her in shock. "You think I'd let a woman who was pregnant with my baby go through the whole thing alone? Of course I didn't know!"

"Of course you didn't." Twenty minutes ago she wouldn't have even asked, but twenty minutes ago she hadn't thought he'd been carrying on with a woman in Aspen, either.

"Listen, can you figure out what to do with her? That crying is tearing me apart."

Matty could see no point in getting angry, but she did anyway. She was furious with this Aspen woman for running away after "parking" her baby. Sebastian's baby. Matty would sacrifice ten years of her life for the chance to be the mother of Sebastian's baby, and the injustice of this situation made her see red.

But somebody had to think clearly in this twosome, and Sebastian didn't appear to be in any shape to do it. "I suggest you bring in the two boxes from the front porch," she said. "My guess is that we'll find supplies in there."

"There were boxes out there?"

"Two of them." She couldn't believe how rattled he was. He wasn't the most observant man in the world, but even he would usually notice two cardboard boxes left on his front porch.

He leaped to the task with obvious eagerness, as if some action, any action, was better than standing around stewing. While he carried them in, plopped them on the floor and ripped into them, Matty finished taking the fleece sleeper off the baby. Sebastian's baby. Every time Matty thought about it, pain stabbed her chest.

Much as she probably ought to, she couldn't leave

the subject alone. "Did she actually say you were the father?"

"No. Her note just asked me to be Elizabeth's godfather until she could come back for her." He crouched beside the boxes, sorting through the contents. "Hey, everything's in here. Formula, diapers, clothes. Even a book on taking care of babies. And there's an envelope." He tore it open and scanned the contents. "Instructions. Birth certificate. Medical records. Some sort of notarized thing giving me permission to have her treated if she gets sick."

Matty's tiny hope that the baby wasn't his began to die. "Sounds as if she means for you to keep her for a while," she said softly.

He didn't acknowledge hearing her. "Okay, here's what she says about feeding. The milk's in cans, and she's already sterilized some bottles and nipples, but she has instructions for how to do it when these run out." Sebastian grabbed up a can and the package of sterilized bottles and nipples. "I'll handle this in the kitchen. Keep rocking her. I think that helps."

"Wash your hands!" Matty called after him. She wasn't sure if rocking helped calm Elizabeth, but it helped calm her. She couldn't imagine what was wrong with this ditzy Aspen woman. Sebastian was the guy to run *to* if you had problems, not *away from*. If he'd accidentally fathered a child, he'd want to do the right thing. If he had any feeling for the mother, or maybe even if he didn't, he'd want to get married and provide the kid with a name and a matched set of parents.

Any woman who didn't realize that, especially after knowing him well enough to make love to him, had to be terminally stupid. She didn't deserve Sebastian or this baby.

He came back in less time than Matty would have expected, but then she remembered Fleafarm's huge litter ten years ago—more pups than faucets. He'd had to fill baby bottles a lot that spring.

He handed her the formula. "Do you know how to do this?"

"I'll muddle through. I don't think it's rocket science." She took the bottle. At first the baby was too upset and refused to latch on, but gradually she seemed to understand what was being offered and accepted the nipple.

Silence.

Except for George Strait singing a love song and the crackling of the fire, both of which reminded Matty of what had been planned for this evening. She hoped the baby had kept things from progressing very far.

Sebastian let out a heavy sigh. Then he picked up the sheaf of instructions and sat down in a wing chair facing Matty. He flipped through the papers and took out one. "She was born on January twenty-ninth, which makes her almost two months old."

Matty didn't have to work very hard to figure it out. Elizabeth had been conceived on or near Sebastian's birthday celebration in Aspen last year. She looked up from the tiny baby to gaze at him. "You're quite a piece of work, you know that?"

"What do you mean?"

"Everybody around here felt so sorry for you because you were having a tough time getting back into the dating game after the divorce. They were so tickled that you finally invited a woman over for *din-*

ner, for crying out loud." Matty hadn't been tickled, but the rest of the valley had seemed overjoyed. "Meanwhile, you've been sowing all sorts of wild oats with some fellow avalanche survivor in Aspen."

He tensed. "I have not been sowing all sorts of wild oats. I'm not even sure I sowed any."

"Then what's this all about?"

His face darkened to a dusky rose. "It's just that I'm not sure. We were all tanked that night, all of us except Jessica."

Jessica. Matty hated the name on principle. "Are you saying you can't remember if you used protection?"

"I can't remember if I made love to her, period."

Matty hated this subject, but she had to know the truth, and she was growing impatient with Sebastian's dense attitude. "Look, you probably did. It was your birthday. It's logical that if you had something going with her, you'd feel like...celebrating."

"That's just it. I *didn't* have something going with her. We're just friends. When you survive something like an avalanche together, you see what people are made of. Jessica has guts." He paused. "Or so I thought."

"Mmm." Matty deliberately kept her response neutral, but a woman with guts didn't desert her baby, in her estimation.

Sebastian seemed to be considering the same subject. Finally he shook his head in bewilderment. "Beats me how she could do this."

"You still haven't explained what happened that might make you the father."

"Well, we really partied that night at the ski lodge—Travis, Boone, Jessica and me. Our avalanche reunion gig, we called it. We'd hoped Nat could make it, but he had some conflict at the last minute. Anyway, Jessica was staying at the lodge, because she works there as a reservation clerk, and we'd rented a cabin nearby, but not close enough to walk. We were so blitzed Jessica drove us home so we wouldn't end up in a snowbank."

"And?"

He blushed even deeper. "Well, you know how it is."

"'Fraid not."

"We were all flirting with her for the hell of it, acting like guys, but it didn't mean anything. At least for me it didn't. She helped each one of us to bed, and I vaguely remember trying to kiss her."

Matty braced herself. "And after the kiss?"

"I don't remember anything after that."

She warned herself not to hope. "Then how can you assume you're the father of this kid?"

"Why else would she ask me to be the godfather?"

"A million reasons." Matty couldn't stem the tide of hope. "You're a good friend. You're steady. You have the resources to handle this sort of responsibility. You're caring. You're gentle. You're—"

"Clueless! I don't know the first thing about babies!"

"So that's why she sent the kid with an instruction manual." Matty felt incredibly lighter. Just friends, he'd said. He couldn't even remember the experience, if there *had* been an experience to remember. Elizabeth wasn't the product of a torrid love affair. At the most, she'd been conceived in a passing moment he couldn't even recall. Matty smiled down at

Elizabeth. Maybe this wasn't such a disaster, after all.

Sebastian watched Matty feeding the baby. She didn't seem completely at ease doing it, but she appeared reasonably competent. Besides that, she looked very nice with that baby in her arms. Softer, somehow. She'd left her blond hair down around her shoulders tonight—that could be part of it. Usually she kept it tied out of the way with a bandanna, or twisted into a single braid.

He'd always thought Matty should have kids, but Butch couldn't have them and he wasn't the kind of guy who'd consider adopting. Butch. Sebastian's gut always tightened when he thought about his late, great neighbor. He'd considered him a good friend. He'd mourned his death after Butch accidentally flew his Cessna into a mountain.

Unfortunately, for her parting shot, Barbara had ruined his memories of Butch by revealing their long-standing affair. Sebastian didn't think Matty knew about that, and he wasn't ever planning to tell her. He wished Barbara had kept the information to herself, except that it made the divorce easier to accept.

Matty had deserved better than Butch, Sebastian thought as she leaned over Elizabeth and looked into the baby's eyes. Matty had the most honest blue eyes he'd ever seen. He'd trust Matty with his life, he realized with some surprise. He'd never thought in those terms before, and it startled him.

He could count on one hand the people he'd place that kind of trust in—Nat Grady, Travis Evans, Boone Conner...and Matty Lang. Not long ago he might have included Jessica in that number, but this baby thing made him wonder if he knew her at all. Leaving a two-month-old child didn't seem to be in character with the Jessica he remembered.

Matty was studying the baby, as if to find some clue about her daddy's identity. Sebastian was plenty curious about the baby's looks, himself. Now that she wasn't all red and screaming, maybe he'd recognize something.

Setting the papers on the lamp table, he got up and walked over to Matty. "Can you tell the color of her eyes?" He hunkered down next to the rocker, balancing himself with one hand on the arm of the chair.

"They could be gray, could be blue. It's hard to tell."

He leaned closer and looked into the baby's eyes. They looked disturbingly familiar. Damn, but they could be the same color as his. This little bundle could be his daughter. His. His stomach twisted. This wasn't the way he pictured bringing a child into the world, abandoned by her mother and thrust upon a father who didn't know what the hell he was doing.

"What color are Jessica's eyes?" Matty asked.

He wrestled his thoughts away from visions of doom.

"Um...let's see. Brown? Maybe brown. I'm not real sure." He liked the way Matty smelled, he thought as he compared her light scent to Charlotte's overpowering perfume. Holding Matty wouldn't force a guy to wear a gas mask. *Holding Matty.* Now there was an intriguing thought. She'd probably knock him from here to kingdom come. Or worse, she'd laugh.

She turned toward him with a smile. "Well, that settles it. You're not carrying a torch for this woman."

"No, I'm not, but why are you suddenly so sure?" It must be the episode with Charlotte that had him thinking crazy. All that kissing earlier in the evening had him looking at Matty's wide, generous mouth and wondering how she'd be to kiss. Talk about crazy. This was Matty, a woman he'd known for ten years. Maybe he was only seeking a distraction from his morbid thoughts about this kid.

"A man in love knows the exact color of his lady's eyes."

"Is that right?" He'd always gotten a kick out of the definite way she put things, as if there could be no doubt in anyone's mind that she was absolutely, positively correct. He could use some of that comforting certainty right now. "And how did you come to learn that particular fact?"

"I read."

"Well, I'm glad to hear that. There's a thick book in that box I'd love to have you dig into."

Her smile faded. "Now, wait a minute, Sebastian."

He muttered a soft curse. "Sorry. That was clumsy. I didn't mean to imply that I expected anything more of you than you've already done."

"Didn't you?"

He sighed and pushed himself upright. "I don't know what I mean. I don't know what I'm going to do." He gestured toward the two boxes. "From the looks of this, Jessica's not coming back tomorrow."

"No, I don't think she is." She hesitated. "Have you considered...taking her to Canon City and...turning her over to—"

"No!"

Elizabeth jerked away from the bottle and started to cry.

"Oh, hell."

"You scared her." Matty tried to get the baby to return to the bottle, but she refused. Hands curled into fists, she beat the air and wailed.

The baby's cries scratched along Sebastian's nerves like fingernails on a chalkboard. He clenched his jaw, feeling helpless and inadequate.

"Maybe she has gas," Matty said. "She probably swallowed a lot of air with all that crying."

"Well, I can tell you this much, she's too damned little for Tums."

"Take the bottle." Matty handed it to him and lifted Elizabeth, positioning her over her shoulder. The baby kept crying as Matty patted and stroked her back.

"Maybe I should hire a nurse." The idea of a strange woman taking up residence in his house depressed the heck out of him, but it might be the only solution.

"Maybe." Matty patted a little harder and gradually Elizabeth stopped crying. Then she let loose with a huge belch.

"My God!" Sebastian stared at the baby.

Matty grinned at him. "Delicate little thing, isn't she?"

"I doubt Travis could make that much noise, and he's put in hours of practice." He smiled back at Matty. He'd become so used to her that he hadn't really looked at her in a long time. But tonight, for some reason, he noticed that she was a pretty woman. Very pretty.

As she held his gaze, her smile faltered. "Listen, maybe you'd rather have a nurse, someone trained to handle a little baby, but I'd be willing...that is, I know I'm not experienced at this, but if you—"

"Are you offering to help me?" He'd never have had the nerve to ask for that kind of commitment. After all, she had as many chores and obligations as he did. But it was what he'd wanted, without fully realizing it, ever since he'd brought the baby into the house. "Because if you are offering, I'm accepting. I don't want a stranger taking care of Elizabeth if you're available."

She took a deep breath and looked straight into his eyes. "I'm available."

He didn't think she'd meant that the way it had sounded. He wouldn't take it the way it sounded, either. Funny, though, how his pulse had picked up at the thought of Matty being...*available*. He was turning into a nutcase. He needed to get a grip before he found himself propositioning every woman he ran across.

He cleared his throat. "Thank you."

3

IF MATTY KNEW any good shrinks, she would be in the market for having her head examined. For two solid years she'd mooned over Sebastian Daniels while he'd remained oblivious. Two years in a row he'd run off to Aspen with the guys for his birthday, and he'd admitted to at least flirting with this woman, even if he hadn't done more than that. Then for his first real date after the divorce, he'd invited Charlotte Crabtree up to the house, not Matty.

Yet all he had to do was look confused and desperate, and good old Matty Lang came running. Still, she wasn't willing to let another woman take care of this abandoned baby, especially if it turned out to be Sebastian's.

"We need to make a plan." She stood, gingerly supporting this unfamiliar bundle against her shoulder, and started toward the dining room. "But first you'd better dig around and find the diaper supplies and the instructions for changing this little girl's britches. I'm sure she must need it by now."

"Where are you taking her?"

"The dining room table's as good a place as any, I guess, although I've never personally changed a diaper. I seem to remember my sister using the dining or kitchen table in a pinch."

His eyes widened. "You've never changed a dia-

per, either? What about with your nieces and nephews?"

"I refused to baby-sit them until they were potty-
trained," she said over her shoulder. "As far as I'm
concerned, kids are more interesting when they can
talk, and when they're old enough to learn to rope
and ride."

Sebastian shook his head as he retrieved the instructions from the lamp table. "I can't believe I've
run across two women in the same evening who
don't know any baby basics. What's this world coming to?"

Matty stopped under the arch dividing the living
room from the dining area and turned back to him.
"Sebastian Daniels, that sounded pretty darned
chauvinistic! I offered to help with this kid, but I'm
sure as heck not going to take over the whole job. If
you're not planning to do at least half the work, then
you'd better hire that nurse you were talking about."

"I'll help, I'll help! Don't get excited, now. I didn't
mean it that way."

"Oh, I think you did. It's very convenient being
helpless at these things, isn't it?"

"Uh—"

"Well, buster, I'm as baby-challenged as you are,
so we'll learn together. And this time, I'll be in
charge of reading the instructions. You can change
the diaper."

He paled. "Me?"

"You'll be doing it soon, anyway." She tried not to
smile. "You might as well figure it out right at the beginning."

"Yeah, but—"

"As my granny used to say, we might as well start

as we mean to go on. And I mean for you to change *at least* half of the diapers." She fixed him with a determined stare, hoping that she looked tough and uncompromising. Inside she was melting at the endearing uncertainty in his eyes, and the worried way he looked at his big hands, as if they weren't adequate to deal with a tiny baby girl.

He took a deep breath. "Okay." He located the box with the diapers inside and tossed the instructions on top before picking up the entire box and carrying it toward the dining room. "Let's do it."

She'd never felt more like hugging him. Then he set the box on the table and flicked on the overhead, and her good will evaporated. For his cozy little dinner with Charlotte he'd used candles, which she'd sort of expected. But she hadn't pictured the vase of store-bought roses sitting in the middle of the table or the good china. And cloth napkins. Damn, he'd gone all out.

"I'll just clear some of this away." Without looking at her, he hastily stacked dishes and carried them into the kitchen.

For the first time, Matty registered that someone was missing from the household. The baby had distracted her, but now that the little tyke was dozing on her shoulder, she could take better stock of the situation. "Where's Fleafarm?" she called into the kitchen.

He came back into the dining room, still looking uncomfortable. "Down in the barn."

"Why?" She had a good idea, but she wanted to see if he'd admit it.

He flushed, and instead of answering, he crossed to the table and grabbed the instructions from the top of the box. "Let's see. She says something about a changing pad. This saddle-blanket thing must be a changing pad." He flopped a quilted pad with ducks and chicks on it across the table's gleaming mahogany surface.

His banishment of his dog made her more indignant than the candles, the roses, the china or the napkins. "What's the matter? Doesn't Charlotte like dogs, either?"

"She, uh, mentioned that a dog could sort of...ruin the mood."

"Go get Fleafarm."

He gestured toward the box. "I thought you wanted me to—"

"I do. You can be back in two minutes. But it's cold in that barn, and Fleafarm is getting on in years. I can't believe you put that poor dog in the barn so that you and Charlotte could play house."

"We didn't do a blasted thing, okay? The baby showed up! And I didn't just drop Fleafarm off at the barn. I made her a real nice bed, with lots of blankets."

So they hadn't had time for the planned hanky-panky. In gratitude Matty cuddled the baby a little closer. "I don't care if you gave that dog twenty blankets. She should be up here at the house. She's a member of the family, dammit. She probably thinks she did something wrong to make you put her out there."

"It's not that all-fired cold." Muttering under his breath, Sebastian stomped back into the kitchen. He crammed his Stetson on his head and went out the back door. But as if to prove his point about the weather, he didn't bother with the sheepskin jacket hanging on a hook by the door.

Matty sighed. "Men." She nuzzled the drowsy baby in her arms. "I can teach you a lot of things, Elizabeth. I can show you how to ride like the wind without falling off, how to quiet a spooky herd of cattle and how to swing the sweetest rope in this valley. But when it comes to men, I don't have a single bit of advice to give you."

Shifting the baby's weight awkwardly so she could pull out a dining room chair, she sat down to wait for that idiot man who was going to freeze his butt to prove a point.

THE NIGHT AIR bit right through Sebastian's shirt and jeans as he hurried down to the barn. Seeing things through Matty's eyes, he felt like a damn fool for making Fleafarm bunk down in the barn. But hell, he hadn't had a date in fourteen years and the process had intimidated him into doing stupid things.

Maybe he should give up on women entirely. Except he didn't really have that option now, not if Elizabeth was his. He had to find Jessica and discover the truth. If he was Elizabeth's father, then he'd talk Jessica into marrying him. He'd had to grow up without both parents around, but he'd be damned if his kid would go through the same thing.

He slid back the bolt and opened the heavy barn door. Instead of turning on a light and getting the horses agitated, he whistled softly for Fleafarm in the darkness.

Tags jingling, she trotted toward him and shoved her wet muzzle in his hand.

"Come on, girl. You've been sprung." He held the

door open for the dog, then closed it securely after her. Fleafarm was of mixed ancestry. She had the rusty coat of a setter, four white socks and a temperament that hinted of a Border collie lurking somewhere in her background, and the body composition of a retriever.

Sebastian had found her wandering on the road, bedraggled and pregnant, eight years ago. Barbara's impulsive nickname had stuck, but Sebastian often wished he'd insisted on a more flattering handle for the animal. Fleafarm was one great dog.

She glanced back at him as if asking for permission to go into the house. With a stab of guilt, he realized Matty had been right. The dog had thought she was being punished.

"Go on. It's okay."

With a little whine of delight, Fleafarm bounded up to the back door and stood there wagging her plume of a tail, her breath making clouds in the cold air. Sebastian felt like a total heel.

And he felt damned cold, too. The warmth of the house wrapped around him like an embrace when he went into the kitchen with Fleafarm. He rubbed his hands together and blew into them.

From the dining room came the sound of Elizabeth fretting. She wasn't crying, thank God, just fussing. Fleafarm stopped dead in her tracks and lifted her floppy ears.

"It's a baby." Sebastian hung his hat on a peg by the door and laid a hand on the dog's head. "Don't reckon you've ever been around one."

Fleafarm gave a sharp little bark and advanced slowly toward the sound that obviously fascinated her.

"Hey, Fleafarm!" Matty called. "Come and say hello to Elizabeth."

The dog moved warily into the dining room. Then she cocked her head and gazed at Matty sitting in a dining room chair, Elizabeth cradled in her arms.

Sebastian had a moment of uneasiness as the dog drew closer. "Do you think it's okay?"

"I think it's essential. You want Fleafarm to be protective of her, don't you?"

He hadn't gotten that far in his thinking. "Does it matter? Elizabeth might only be here a few days."

"She might." Matty glanced at him. "Or she might be here a whole lot longer. Unless Jessica mentioned a specific time frame for this caper?"

"Not exactly. The note only said she wanted me to be a godfather to Elizabeth until she could return for her."

"Which leaves this operation completely open-ended. You'd better prepare yourself for more than a few days. I'm not sure you realize yet that your life has just been turned upside down."

"Oh, it's beginning to sink in."

"Good. Facing reality is admirable." Matty watched the dog edge closer. "It's okay, Fleafarm. You've been a mommy, so you know about babies. This is like a puppy, only bigger. And less hair." She glanced up at Sebastian. "Maybe you should come on over here and pet Fleafarm while she gets used to the idea of this baby. We don't want jealousy getting in the way of bonding. And we don't want Fleafarm to slobber over Elizabeth and scare her to death."

Sebastian walked over and scratched the dog behind her ears. Then he crouched down and wrapped an arm around the silky neck, restraining her gently.

The dog's coat was cold, and Sebastian was still shivering from his jaunt outside, but he worked to control it so Matty wouldn't have cause to say she told him so.

He turned to the dog. "You wouldn't be jealous of that little baby, would you Fleafarm?"

She whined and licked his face.

"Oh, yes, she would," Matty said. "But if you make sure she knows you still love her, she'll probably guard this baby with her life. At least that's the way it worked with my nieces and nephews and the dogs they had. You have to make sure you don't appear to be giving more attention to Elizabeth than you do to Fleafarm."

"This sure is getting complicated."

Matty looked into his eyes. "You still have a choice."

He gazed back at her. "No, I don't."

Elizabeth made a soft, cooing sound, like a dove on a summer morning.

Sebastian glanced at the baby in surprise and pleasure. Now there was a noise he could grow fond of.

Elizabeth stared at the dog and her little fists waved in the air. For the first time Sebastian admitted she was sort of cute, with her fuzzy crop of light-colored hair and round baby face. She cooed again.

Fleafarm whined and wagged her tail.

"Love at first sight," Matty pronounced.

"No such thing," Sebastian said. He wasn't even sure what love was, period. He'd thought he was in love with Barbara, but she hadn't been in love with him, at least not for very long—and certainly not when she was carrying on with Butch for all those years.

"Maybe love at first sight is rare for people, but for dogs and kids, it happens all the time." Matty leaned down and kissed Elizabeth on the cheek. "Well, I think that's enough dog-baby communication for the time being." She picked up Elizabeth and cradled her against her shoulder. Then she turned her face toward the baby and gave her another kiss. "We can work on it later, okay, sweetheart? Right now I know a little girl who needs her diaper changed."

"I was hoping you'd done it while I was out getting the dog."

Matty grinned. "I'm sure you were. You'd better go wash your hands, and use hot water to warm them up. No lady likes to be touched with cold hands."

Damned if that comment didn't get him to thinking of touching Matty, which he'd done before, but only as a friend. Now he was wondering how it would be to touch her like a lover.

She'd said Fleafarm might be jealous of the attention the baby was getting. Well, Sebastian found himself mighty jealous of the way Matty was cuddling Elizabeth, giving her kisses and nuzzling her. He'd never known Matty to be so openly affectionate, but then he'd never seen her with a baby, either.

He wondered if she'd been playful and snuggly with Butch when the two of them had been alone. If she had been that open and vulnerable, his heart ached for her, because she'd been married to a faithless man.

"Oh, don't scowl like that." Matty laughed. "I doubt if changing a diaper is going to be any worse than mucking out a stall."

"Says you, the person who has no more experience than I have." He wiped the frown off his face and was glad she'd misinterpreted it. Pushing himself to his feet, he clucked to Fleafarm and got her settled under the table, one of her favorite spots.

"Don't worry," Matty said. "You'll be a diapering fool in no time."

"That's what I'm afraid of."

She gazed at him. "Are you worried that you'll ruin your macho reputation with the guys?"

He grimaced, and her soft laughter taunted him as he headed into the kitchen to wash up. To be honest, he hadn't thought of himself as doing this sort of chore if he ever became a parent.

With her usual dexterity, Matty had exposed another uncomfortable truth about Sebastian Daniels. Whenever he'd imagined being a father, he'd sort of skipped the baby stage in his mind. He'd pictured buying the kid a pony, helping with homework, flying kites. He hadn't pictured changing diapers. Apparently he'd unconsciously assigned baby care to the mother. Not very enlightened.

Well, Matty wouldn't let him get away with being unenlightened. He smiled as he soaped up and ran warm water over his chilled hands. Matty wouldn't let him get away with a damn thing. He realized he'd always counted on her to tell him the truth, and at the moment he needed the truth more than anything else. He needed Matty. Thank God she'd offered to help him.

They hadn't figured out any details yet, though. This little bundle of joy would need looking after twenty-four hours a day, and he'd feel much better if both of them were on hand, at least at first. He wondered if Matty would consider staying over until they'd established some workable routine.

Yeah, that was the answer. The three of them needed to stick together for a while. They could all drive over to Matty's place and do her feeding and chores, then come back here and do his. This time of year the main job was making sure fences were ready for the yearlings they'd buy in May. His fences were in decent shape, and he could help Matty with hers if she needed some repairs done. In fact, it'd be sort of fun having Matty around all the time. He began to whistle under his breath.

IN THE DINING ROOM, Matty laid Elizabeth on the changing pad. Sebastian's tuneless whistle drifted in from the kitchen, teasing her nerve endings. She was beginning to question the wisdom of her impulsive offer. Only one course of action made sense, for her to stay over at the Rocking D until they came up with a regular schedule for the baby.

On the surface it wasn't a difficult proposition. Getting the work done on both ranches wouldn't be a problem. Until they bought the cattle in May, they only had to fix fences and take care of the horses. Her dog Sadie got along fine with Fleafarm. Sebastian had a spare bedroom.

But every time Matty thought of sleeping here, of sharing every meal and every waking hour with Sebastian, her stomach churned. With that much togetherness, he would eventually figure out that she had a huge, incurable crush on him.

For years, she'd hidden it successfully behind a tough ranch-woman facade, but caring for this tiny baby would make that a hard act to maintain. Already she'd felt unexpected longings as she cradled the helpless infant in her arms. Maybe the reason she'd refused to take care of her nieces and nephews when they were babies was that she'd subconsciously known it would be a painful reminder that she had no babies of her own.

Sebastian came into the dining room, his hands held high as if he'd scrubbed for surgery. "My gown, nurse."

As she gazed at his strong, hair-sprinkled forearms and capable hands, hands she'd dreamed would someday touch her with tenderness, funny things happened to her heart. "Smart aleck," she said, and grinned because he expected that. But she was so afraid everything she was feeling shone in her eyes that she glanced away. "Come on over here and take hold of this kid so I can start reading up on how we accomplish this. We don't want her falling on the floor when we're not paying attention."

"Oh, God." He blanched and hurried over to the table. "Maybe we should just do it on the floor so there's no chance we'll drop her." He moved in close, hip-to-hip with Matty.

"Yeah, down there with the dog hair and the bread crumbs. That'd be super." She put an inch or so of space between them. After the way she'd been thinking a moment ago, body contact wasn't a good thing. She maintained her sisterly tone of voice with difficulty. "You do a decent job of cleaning for a guy, but I wouldn't want to put a baby on your floor. The table's fine if we keep track of her. Here, put your hand on her chest and keep it there while I get the instructions."

Sebastian settled a tentative hand on Elizabeth,

who stared up at him without blinking. "I wonder if she knows that we're greenhorns at this diapering business?" he said.

"If she doesn't know now, she will soon enough." Satisfied that Sebastian had Elizabeth secured on the table, Matty moved away and picked up the typed list of instructions. She had to give Jessica points for thoroughness. She must have been somewhat concerned about the kid to go to all this trouble.

Matty scanned the pages until she found the section on diapering. "Okay, we've got her on the changing pad on a flat surface and we're making sure she doesn't roll off. Now unsnap the sleeper gizmo so you can take it off the bottom half of her."

Sebastian started fumbling with the small snaps with his free hand. He blew out a breath. "I can't do it with one hand. Would it bother your feminist sensibilities to help with this one part?"

"I guess not." But it played hell with her hormones to move in close enough to smell his citrus aftershave and feel the warmth of his body close beside her. She put down the instructions and concentrated on the snaps as best she could, considering that all she wanted was to snuggle against him and feel those strong arms around her.

"Why does she keep staring at me like that?" he asked.

Because all females do, you lunkhead. You're gorgeous. "She's probably trying to figure out who the heck you are."

"I think she has my eyes."

"You know what? I'm not so sure." She didn't want to believe that Sebastian had made love to Jessica, even if he couldn't remember the incident. She hurried on with the instructions. "Now you *carefully* unfasten the tabs on the diaper and *slowly* take it off, because—" Matty started to giggle.

"Because?" Sebastian prompted.

She spoke around the laughter choking her up. "It says here that you never know what you're going to find and you need to contain whatever you encounter." She wiped her eyes and chuckled. "I'll say this for your Aspen friend. She has a wry sense of humor."

"Oh, she's a laugh a minute, dropping babies on doorsteps like this," he muttered as he worked at the tabs on the diaper. "Can you come over here and put a hand on this little girl while I wrestle with these tab things? I can see right off this is a two-person job."

Matty did as he requested, which made them very chummy, their bodies bumping against each other, his warm breath on her neck, his elbow nudging her breast. She tried to remain oblivious and failed.

"What's that perfume you're wearing?"

"Wh-what?" She couldn't believe his thoughts had been anywhere near hers.

"What kind is it?"

"I forget the name." Her heart pounded. "It's supposed to smell like jasmine. Why?"

"I like it."

"Oh." She tried to tell herself that it didn't matter one way or the other. He was making idle conversation. But what if he wasn't?

"There, it's off." He sighed with relief. "We lucked out. It's just wet."

She laughed, feeling giddy from his comment about her cologne. "I don't think your luck will hold forever on that score, cowboy."

"Probably not. What's next?"

She glanced at the set of instructions she'd forgotten she clutched in her hand. "Roll up the diaper and dispose of it later. Then clean her with a baby wipe."

"Where's that?"

"Hold onto her." Matty extricated herself. "I think I saw them in the box."

"Can you imagine me doing this all by myself? I would have killed her by now."

She found the baby wipes, pulled one out of the container and handed it to him. "No, you wouldn't, but it does seem to take both of us to replace one experienced mother."

"That's what I've been thinking." He leaned over Elizabeth. "Hold still there, little one."

Watching him tend to the baby with such gentleness made Matty's throat tighten. He was going to be one hell of a daddy, if it turned out this little bundle belonged to him.

"Matty, do you think you could see your way clear to stick around here for the next few days?" he asked casually, not looking at her as he continued to work on Elizabeth.

Her heartbeat quickened. Although she'd been expecting the request, she wasn't ready with her answer.

"I know it'll be a pain in the neck," he continued, still concentrating on the baby. "But I don't see how else we can manage this. We can bring Sadie over here, of course, and I'll help you take care of things at your place. We could drive over a couple of times a day. If you've got fence to mend, I'll be happy to help you with it." In the silence, he glanced up at her. "You're being mighty quiet."

"I'm thinking."

A coaxing light came into his gray eyes. "I really need you here, Matty. I'd be petrified to be left alone with this baby right here at the beginning."

As if she ever could have denied him. When he looked at her like that, she'd give him anything he wanted, including her heart. "Okay," she said. "I'll stay over."

4

MATTY WOULD STAY. Sebastian almost keeled over in relief. The seemingly impossible job of dealing with this baby had been whittled down to a workable size.

"I think Elizabeth's ready for her diaper," he said with newfound confidence. He held out his hand. "Lay one on me."

Matty gave him one from the box. "Go to it."

Sebastian took the folded diaper and spread it on the table with one hand while he kept the other on Elizabeth's chest. "Seems easy enough. We'll just work in reverse. All we have to do is—"

Elizabeth squealed and started to kick and wave her arms.

"Hey!" The diaper slipped from his fingers onto the floor as he grabbed the baby with both hands. "Now is not the time to learn boot-scootin', Elizabeth!"

The baby stared up at him and gurgled. Then she made that soft little cooing sound he liked so much.

A knot of anxiety loosened inside Sebastian's gut when he heard the happy little noise, the same one she'd made when she'd seen his dog for the first time. Apparently she could tolerate the idea of having a cowboy like him take care of her. Secretly he'd been worried about that. Just because Jessica had decided to leave the baby with him didn't mean the baby would like it much.

"I think you've made a friend," Matty said softly.

He was embarrassed by how pleased that made him, so he minimized the significance of it. "Yeah, any friend of Fleafarm's is a friend of hers."

As if in response, the dog nudged his leg. Sebastian glanced down to see Fleafarm standing patiently beside him, the fallen diaper held delicately in her mouth.

"Oh, my God," Matty said. "That is beyond cute."

Fleafarm wagged her tail and looked up at them expectantly.

"Good dog!" Matty rubbed behind Fleafarm's ears. "Thank you so much." She took the diaper. "Now go lie down. That's a good girl."

"We're not using a diaper that is covered with dog slobber, are we?"

"Pretend like you're using it," Matty said out of the corner of her mouth. "Don't hurt her feelings by rejecting her offer of help."

Sebastian sighed and took the diaper. "As life gets ever more complicated." Then he made his tone bright. "Look, Elizabeth! Fleafarm picked up your diaper. The diaper we are going to use to cover your cute little tush. This very diaper. Absolutely. This one." He shoved it into the middle of the table and grabbed the new one Matty slipped quietly to him.

About that time Elizabeth started kicking and cooing again. "Damn, how does anybody do this all by themselves?"

"I seem to remember my sister had a strap on her changing table. And a mobile hanging over it, to distract the kid. Let me see if I can help keep her occupied." Matty moved around him, leaned down toward the baby and spoke in a low voice. "Now, Elizabeth, if you'll stay very, very quiet, I'll tell you a deep, dark secret. Something not very many people know. But you have to promise never, ever to breathe a word of this to anyone. Promise?"

Sebastian hadn't ever heard Matty use that tone of voice. It sounded almost seductive, like the sort of tone a woman might use during lovemaking. He wondered if that's the way Matty sounded when she—

"Sebastian?" She glanced up at him. "I'm trying to hypnotize this kid, not you. Get busy."

"Oh. Yeah. Right." He snatched up the diaper. "I'm on it."

"This secret is about the owner of that well-known spread, the Rocking D Ranch," Matty continued.

Sebastian didn't know how he was supposed to concentrate on diapering this baby when Matty was talking about him in that tone of voice, but he struggled along.

"It seems on a very hot day last summer, this owner of the Rocking D went fishing for trout."

"Some secret," Sebastian mumbled. "I fish for trout every summer."

"Naked as a jaybird," Matty whispered to the baby.

Sebastian's head jerked up. "You can't know about that!"

"Oh, but I do." She slanted a glance at him, laughter dancing in her eyes.

Heat crept up from his collar. "Travis or Boone saw me and told you about it."

"Nope."

"Matty Lang! You spied on me?"

She started laughing in earnest and turned back to the baby. "You know what else, Elizabeth?"

The baby crowed and gurgled, obviously getting into the spirit of the moment.

Sebastian looked at his work and discovered that in his agitation he'd taped the diaper tab to his forearm. "I don't think Elizabeth needs to hear any more secrets."

"Are you finished yet?" Matty asked smugly.

"Almost." He winced as he pulled the tape off and ripped out a few hairs in the process.

"Then I need to keep her entertained a little longer, don't I?" She lowered her voice into that sexy register again. "You see, Elizabeth, this certain rancher likes to serenade the fish. He swears it brings them to his line. So there he was, standing in the stream in his birthday suit, singing *Ghost Riders in the Sky*, when the biggest trout you've ever seen in your life leaped right up between his legs. My theory is that it was attracted by the dangling—"

"I can't *believe* you hid in the trees like some bushwacker and saw all that!" Sebastian figured he was red enough by now to stop traffic. "So how many people have you entertained with that little story?"

"Just one. And you're safe until she learns how to talk."

If Sebastian had been all thumbs before, he might as well have been trying to put on the diaper with his toes now. He fumbled and swore under his breath. "And what were you doing sneaking around through the trees when a man was trying to have some private time fishing?"

"Who knew it was supposed to be *that* private? I was just taking a walk."

"A walk?" The concept was totally foreign to him. "Likely story. Cowboys don't walk. They ride."

"I'm not a cowboy."

"You know what I meant."

She sighed with disappointment. "Unfortunately, I do."

"What's that supposed to mean?"

"Nothing. I know what you meant, that's all."

He glanced at her. "You're a good hand, Matty. You ride as well as any man I know, and you rope better than most. Not a lot of women can say that."

She met his gaze. "True. I'll bet Charlotte Crabtree can't say it."

"Are you kidding?" His short laugh made Elizabeth jerk under his hand, and he stroked her tummy the way he would the soft nose of a skittish filly. "Charlotte would be lucky to stay on a horse that moved any faster than a slow amble. Charlotte's not what you'd call an outdoorsy type."

"Then why did you invite her out here to dinner?"

Red was becoming his permanent look. "To... um...well, to..."

"Never mind," Matty said, her voice softer. "I know why. And it's none of my business. Please forget I asked."

He couldn't get over the feeling that inviting Charlotte out to dinner had diminished him in Matty's eyes. He didn't like being diminished where Matty was concerned. "It wasn't like that!"

"Sure it was. Exactly like that. It's okay, Sebastian. You're a grown man. You're entitled to sexual activity."

And she was a grown woman, he thought as he gazed at her. Wasn't she entitled to sexual activity, too? And yet he'd never thought about that. He'd never considered that she might be lonely, or have unfulfilled sexual needs. Maybe he'd assumed that Butch's affair with Barbara had started because Matty wasn't a very passionate woman to begin with.

But that wasn't a fair assumption to make. Butch could have been one of those people who needed more than one sexual relationship at a time. Apparently Barbara was like that. In fact, she'd told him she didn't intend to remarry, because she didn't like being tied to one man. Monogamy didn't work for everyone.

Pink tinged Matty's cheeks and she glanced away. "I don't know how we got off on that subject." She brought her attention back to Elizabeth. "You seem to have put that on her, more or less."

"Guess so." He studied the diapering job. It wasn't neat. One leg looked a little too tight and the other one seemed loose. One tab, the one he'd stuck to his arm, wasn't particularly secure, but they'd already wasted a diaper and he figured this one would hold well enough to get them to the next diapering session.

"Why don't you snap her back into her sleeper?" Matty suggested.

"Okay." Sebastian tucked one tiny foot into the leg of the sleeper and started redoing the snaps. No doubt about it, he felt more comfortable with the routine than he had a few minutes ago. He could even work around Elizabeth's gyrations without going into a panic.

"We should figure out a place where she can sleep temporarily until you buy her a crib," Matty said.

"A *crib?*" That sounded way too permanent for his tastes. "I can't believe we have to worry about a crib."

Matty gazed at him. "I still don't think you've figured this out. Elizabeth was delivered with detailed instructions and a ton of supplies. Her mother went to a considerable amount of trouble to see that she was set up well. I can't believe she did all that work so that you could fill in for a couple of days."

"Well, then maybe for a week." He finished the last of the snaps and laid his hand over the baby's chest to steady her on the table. "There's no point in buying a bunch of baby furniture if she's only going to be here a week."

"But you don't know for sure how long she'll be here. I'd also suggest a changing table. It would make a huge difference when we're diapering her. As for the crib, you could make-do with a drawer or a wash basket, but if it were me, I'd worry about her getting a splinter or somehow falling out. I'd feel a lot better if you bought a crib."

Sebastian resisted the whole idea. Baby furniture in the house seemed like an admission that he'd indeed fathered this child in a wild and irresponsible act, an act that violated all his principles. He stroked the baby while he talked. "I still say it doesn't make sense until I know for sure Elizabeth is mine."

"I say it does, and I'm the one helping you with her, so I get a vote, too. Even if she's not yours, you could save the furniture for when you do have kids of your own."

"That might never happen." The admission made him sad, but he had to face facts.

"That would be a crying shame. I know how you've always wanted them, and you'd make a great father."

He continued to rub Elizabeth's tummy, and she lay still, her eyes drifting closed. "Yeah, well, I'm almost thirty-five years old, and I don't even have a girlfriend, let alone a wife. Maybe I wasn't meant to have a family."

"Sebastian, are you feeling sorry for yourself?" She sounded a little impatient.

"No." But he was. Ten years ago he'd thought he had his life figured out. He and Barbara would raise a family on this ranch and then they'd grow old together. One of the kids would take over when he got too decrepit to manage the chores. Except that he discovered Barbara didn't want kids, and she didn't much want a ranch once she'd understood the work it entailed.

"You are so feeling sorry for yourself." There was a definite snap to Matty's voice. "And for no reason. Women around here are constantly trying to get you to notice them."

"They are not."

"They are, too! Unfortunately for them, you're one of the most oblivious men I've ever met when it comes to that. Sooner or later, one of those women will get through to you, though, and before you know it, you'll be walking down the aisle of the Huerfano Community Church. It's just a matter of time. You're probably the only one in this valley who thinks you're headed for a lonely old age."

"Thanks for settling my mind on that score." He

couldn't think of any women in the valley he'd want to marry, but maybe she was right, and he hadn't looked hard enough.

He couldn't help wondering what sort of old age she pictured for herself. Women's lib aside, single women still didn't have the opportunities to find a new mate the way men did, especially out here in the country. "Have you had a date? I mean since Butch died."

"One." She busied herself with the diaper supplies. "Go ahead and pick her up."

First of all he wanted to know about that one date, and second of all he didn't want to pick up Elizabeth. He decided to deal with the second matter. "I don't know how to hold her."

Her gaze flicked to his. "Now's a fantastic time to learn. She's practically asleep, so she'll be easier to handle."

"I might wake her up and she'll start screaming again."

"I doubt it. She's fed and changed, and you've been stroking her so nicely I'll bet she's perfectly relaxed and happy."

Sebastian looked doubtfully at the little pink bundle on the table. Her eyes were closed and her mouth formed a small circle, like baby dolls he'd seen in the department store at Christmastime. She lay so still she could have been one of those dolls, except for the gentle rise and fall of her chest and the occasional flutter of an eyelash. She terrified him.

"Scoop one hand under her butt and the other one under her head and neck," Matty said. "I remember my sisters saying babies this young can't support the weight of their heads, especially when they're relaxed like this."

"You do it."

"Nope." Matty put her hands on her hips. "Your turn."

Sebastian almost smiled. He'd seen that defiant gesture a thousand times, at least. Although he'd never known Butch and Matty to cuddle, he'd seen them square off against each other, and Matty had always held her ground. Most of the time he'd mentally sided with her in the argument, but in the interests of friendship he'd stayed out of their disputes. For the first time it occurred to him that Matty might not have been happy in that marriage, even though she'd always put a good face on things.

She gestured toward Elizabeth. "Go ahead. We can't very well let her sleep on the table."

A bead of sweat trickled down his spine. Man, he didn't want to do this. Changing her while Matty stayed right there and made sure she didn't roll off was one thing. But if he picked her up, a million things could go wrong. He could drop her, or bend her in some way she wasn't supposed to bend, or squeeze her too tight. He wasn't good with tiny, delicate stuff. Barbara had forbidden him to wash or dry her imported crystal.

But Matty had logic and fairness on her side in demanding that he do this. He liked to think he was a fair man. Taking a deep breath, he worked one hand under Elizabeth's bottom. She moved her pink lips in a sucking motion but didn't open her eyes.

"That's it," Matty said gently. "Now support her head and shoulders with the other hand."

That was the tricky part, he thought. He eased his

hand under her head, marveling at the softness of her downy hair against his palm. She opened her eyes. "Go back to sleep," he murmured, hoping he didn't sound as desperate as he felt.

She blinked once and closed her eyes again, as if obeying his orders.

Matty chuckled. "Don't expect that kind of obedience all the time. I think she's exhausted."

"So am I. And I'm a nervous wreck, besides," he added, hoping she might take pity on him and offer to carry the baby, after all.

"Poor Sebastian."

"You're not gonna cut me any slack on this, are you?"

"Nope."

He remembered hauling hurt cowboys out of the rodeo arena, and he decided to treat lifting Elizabeth the same way. Carefully sliding his wrist under her, he was able to support both her head and neck. With a silent prayer, he lifted her from the table and held her suspended in midair, his elbows braced against his ribs for stability.

She didn't wake up.

He held himself rigid. "I've got her. Now where do you want me to take her?"

"Into your bedroom."

"Okay." He turned, keeping his arms out in the same position so he wouldn't wiggle her.

Matty giggled.

"Shh!"

"Sorry, but you look like you're a butler serving hors d'oeuvres. Bring her in a little closer to your body."

"How?"

"Like this." Matty grasped his right arm. "Hey, your muscles are all tensed up."

"That's because *I'm* all tensed up."

"Well, loosen up your arm, and let's position her head in the crook of your elbow." She guided him into the position she wanted.

Her touch felt reassuring. Actually more energizing than reassuring. He could smell that light floral fragrance again, and the scent of recently shampooed hair. Warmth moved through him and settled pleasantly in his groin. He wasn't exactly aroused, but he was in the pre-arousal stage, when all he'd need to do was tip her face up to his and kiss her, and he'd be aroused.

Not that he would do such a thing. This was Matty he was talking about, and besides, he had his arms full of baby Elizabeth.

"There." Matty stepped back, as if surveying a weaving she'd completed. "Better."

Sebastian gazed down at the sleeping bundle cradled against his chest. Elizabeth rested quietly, as if she knew he would keep her safe. Her silent, unquestioning faith did something funny to his insides. His throat tightened. He didn't know how he'd won her trust, but he vowed he would never, ever betray it.

Matty watched Sebastian holding the sleeping baby and her eyes moistened. When she'd helped him rearrange Elizabeth in his arms, she'd fought the almost overwhelming urge to wrap her arms around man and child, hugging them close. She longed to lay her head against Sebastian's solid shoulder and create, if only for a moment, the precious family unit she'd dreamed of. God, how she ached.

She'd imagined this scene so many times, except in her fantasy Sebastian would be holding their baby. He'd gaze down at the tiny infant as he was doing now, and then he'd look up, speechless with wonder, love filling his gray eyes.

She couldn't bear to have the fantasy ruined by whatever comment he might make, so she broke the mood herself. "Bring her in the bedroom," she said as she started toward the back of the house. "I'll empty out one of your dresser drawers. Then we can put a blanket in for her."

"Use the bottom one," he said. "It's got some old sweaters and sweatshirts in it, and it's the deepest."

"Okay." She walked into the bedroom, intent on her purpose until she saw the mussed sheets. Sebastian wouldn't have left his bed unmade if he was having guests, which meant that the sheets had been disturbed after the guest arrived. She stood there looking at the rumpled bed and a knot of pure jealousy formed in her stomach.

Sebastian came in the room and glanced from Matty to the bed. "Nothing happened."

Matty swallowed. "It's not my business whether it did or not." Jaw clenched, she stomped over to the dresser.

"Charlotte came in here when the doorbell rang." He sounded defensive. "I guess she climbed in."

"Goodness, I wonder why she'd do a thing like that?" Matty crouched down and pulled open the bottom drawer of the old pine dresser. She'd always loved Sebastian and Barbara's bedroom furniture. They'd found it at a fleamarket in Canon City, and it had the aged look Matty thought was perfect for a ranch-house bedroom.

"There's no need to get sarcastic."

"You're right. I apologize." Matty was embarrassed by her violent reaction to the bedroom scene. She might as well announce to Sebastian that she was pea-green with envy. She started pulling his sweaters and sweatshirts out of the drawer and piling them in her arms. The scent of outdoors and citrus that always clung to Sebastian drifted up from the pile of clothes tucked in her arm. She wanted to bury her nose in the soft fabric.

"Charlotte was a bad choice." He stood watching her unload the drawer. "I shouldn't have invited her out here. But I figured I should start somewhere."

Despair washed over her. He'd never considered his next-door neighbor. Matty had never even crossed his mind. She'd kidded herself that he wasn't ready yet, and that's why he'd never approached her. But he was ready. She pulled the last sweater from the drawer to discover a box of condoms underneath. Boy, was he ready.

"Oh. Uh, I forgot I put those down there."

She plopped the box on top of the stack of clothes and stood. "As I said, you're a grown man. Where do you want this stuff?"

He looked very uncomfortable. "On the chair over by the window is fine."

"Okay." She turned and carried the clothes and the offending box to the ladder-backed chair by the window.

He followed her over there. "Listen, Matty, I know what this seems like, with me holding a baby who could be mine, and you finding solid evidence of what was likely to happen here tonight with Charlotte, but you're getting the wrong picture. I'm not—"

"Interested in sex?" She set the clothes down and the box slid to the floor. She picked it up and placed it carefully on top of the pile. She even aligned it so it was straight.

"Of course I'm interested in sex."

Just not with me. She didn't look at him. The muted light in the bedroom, the rumpled sheets and the sound of his voice was getting to her. If Elizabeth hadn't been there, she would have made a complete fool of herself.

"The truth is, I haven't had sex since Barbara left, with the possible exception of that night in Aspen, which I can't even remember. So, in a way, that doesn't even count."

"Don't feel obliged to explain yourself to me, Sebastian." She went back to the dresser. If she kept moving, she might avoid letting him know that she was interested in sex with him, anytime, anyplace. She reached for the drawer and started wrestling it loose.

"Do you need help with that?"

"Nope." She kept tugging, but the dresser was old and the drawers sometimes stuck.

"Here, you take the baby and let me do that."

"Never mind. I've got it." The last thing she needed was to get cozy with him while they exchanged the baby. Teeth clenched, she gave a mighty pull. The drawer came out and she landed hard on her butt on the wooden floor.

"Now, see that? You probably bruised yourself, maybe even cracked something."

"I'm fine." Still holding the drawer, she got to her

feet, determined not to wince. "Are the extra blankets still in the hall closet?"

"Yes, they are." He followed her into the hall. "You know, Matty, you are the most stubborn, independent female I've ever run across."

"I doubt that." Matty thought of Barbara, who had been stubborn in her own way. She'd hated ranch work and had simply stopped doing it.

"You are completely stubborn." Sebastian's tone was not complimentary. "You would rather risk hurting yourself than ask for help, wouldn't you?"

She turned from the closet, a soft blanket clutched against her chest. Then she gazed at him as the accusation shot home, along with a burst of insight.

He was absolutely right. She was terrible at asking for anything. And the way he put it, she could understand why he'd never considered rolling with her over that unmade bed. She was an idiot for not figuring it out earlier. He wasn't attracted to her because she was too self-sufficient. And she didn't think she could change that for anyone, not even Sebastian.

5

MATTY PUT THE blanket-padded drawer in the middle of Sebastian's bed, and by some miracle he managed to shovel Elizabeth into it without waking her. Then they had to decide where to put the drawer.

"In the guest room, where you'll be, is the logical place." He grasped the sides of the drawer and started to lift it from the bed.

Matty laid a restraining hand on his arm. "Wrong. This isn't a gender-based decision. I'm only the helper, remember? Jessica left her kid with you, not me. The drawer goes in your room. You can put it on the floor by the bed." She pointed to a spot on the braided rug.

Sebastian eyed the spot and rubbed the back of his neck. "Except I won't be in here to watch her. I have to go fetch Sadie and some clothes for you."

She gaped at him. "Why on earth would you be the one to do that? I'll go get Sadie and my clothes. In fact, I might as well leave right now."

His agitation grew. "I think I should go. You can stay here with her while I run over and get your stuff."

"That's plain silly."

He sighed. Matty's logic was winning the argument. "Okay, it's silly. But...the truth is I don't feel right being alone with her yet."

"She'll probably sleep the whole time." Matty gazed at him. "It'll be good practice for you. You have to get used to taking care of this kid, eventually, Sebastian. I'll only be gone a little while. Thirty minutes, tops. You can handle it." She started out of the room.

He grabbed her arm. "Wait."

She turned, her lips parted as if in protest.

For a split second he wondered what would happen if he pulled her close and kissed that wide, generous mouth of hers. He'd been wanting to do it ever since she arrived tonight. That would take her mind off leaving him in the lurch. But she'd probably think he was completely crazy, not to mention sex-starved, so sex-starved he'd hit on his neighbor and best friend.

So he released her arm. "Let me run over to your place. I'll be glad to try staying alone with Elizabeth tomorrow, but after going through hell alone tonight while she lay there and screamed, I'm feeling kinda raw. I don't think I could face anymore of that right now."

"So what if I'm here alone and she screams?"

"It wouldn't scare you the way it did me."

She surveyed him quietly for a long moment. "Bring her out in the living room, then, and I'll stay here. We'll move her into your room when we go to bed."

He wasn't comfortable with that idea, either, but at least he was temporarily off the hook. "I appreciate it more than you know." He picked up the drawer and followed her down the hall.

"I'll make a list of what to bring over for tonight.

The rest we can worry about tomorrow when we go feed the horses."

"Okay. Should I put Elizabeth by the rocking chair?"

"That's fine." She paused. "You know, I always wondered where that chair came from. It doesn't look like something Barbara would choose."

"It was my grandmother's, and I remembered it from when I was a kid. When she died, I asked for it." He'd had some idea Barbara would like it, but she hadn't taken to the chair or the idea of rocking babies, for that matter.

"It's a great chair," Matty said. "Well, I'd better go make that list for you."

As Matty went into the kitchen in search of paper and pencil, Sebastian gazed after her, touched that she liked the rocker. Once again he had the urge to draw her into his arms. Must be gratitude working on him.

Then again maybe not. Maybe he was finally seeing what a fine woman Matty was. He set the drawer next to the rocker and sat down. He leaned his head against the back and rocked slowly, thinking about the way he was reacting to Matty, compared to the way he'd reacted to Charlotte.

Although Charlotte was attractive and he'd been turned on, the evening had felt more like an exercise than the joyous occasion it should have been. Still, Charlotte had done him a favor by getting his mind running on that track again. Now that it was, he saw Matty in a whole new light.

But he hadn't the foggiest idea what to do about it, if he did anything at all. First off, he didn't know how a guy made a move on a no-nonsense woman like Matty. She wasn't the candlelight, wine and roses type, and all his old techniques and lines seemed silly when applied to her. Besides, if he went so far as to kiss her, what then? He was risking a lot. They needed each other as neighbors and friends, and if he screwed that up so they felt awkward with each other, they'd both lose out.

"I think that should do it." She came into the living room with the piece of scratch paper she'd found in the kitchen.

He stood and walked over to take her list. It was short, which didn't surprise him. Matty didn't fuss with herself, which might be one of the reasons he'd never thought of her in sexual terms. She didn't do anything to call attention to her womanly charms. But somehow the baby had done that for her, and now he couldn't seem to think of anything *but* her womanly charms.

She'd noted where everything was that he needed to pick up, but he probably could have found it, anyway. They were both familiar with each other's homes and living habits.

"Want a book?" he asked. She always took at least one on roundup and read by the light of the fire before going to sleep. She'd sit on a stump, her blanket around her shoulders and her golden hair catching the light from the fire as she sat totally absorbed in some fictional world. He'd liked watching her while he pretended to be asleep. He'd never realized how much he treasured that mental picture of Matty reading by the campfire.

"I doubt I'll need it tonight," she said. "But sure, just in case insomnia strikes. The one I'm reading is on my bedside table."

"Who did you have the date with?"

She looked confused.

"The date," he reminded her. "I asked if you'd had a date since Butch died, and you said you'd had one. I was wondering, although he never said anything, if you dated Travis."

Matty grinned. "No. I may be the only woman in the valley Travis hasn't dated, but the truth is, there's no chemistry between us. We've even talked about it. He said that was one of the main reasons he decided to take the head wrangler job at the Leaning L. Neither of us would be tempted to do something stupid and louse up a good working relationship."

"Makes sense." Sebastian was relieved. Travis was a good friend, and he'd rather not have a good friend dating Matty. "So who was it?"

She hesitated only a moment before giving a little shrug. "I went to the movies with Cyrus from the feed store."

"Cyrus?" Heated indignation rushed through him at the thought of that young stud going out with Matty. "Isn't that robbing the cradle? He can't be a day over twenty-three."

A dangerous light came into her eyes. "He's twenty-seven, and you'd better watch yourself. Charlotte Crabtree just turned thirty, and I'll bet you didn't even consider the difference in your ages when you asked her out."

Damn. He'd been caught with his hand in the sexist cookie jar again. He cleared his throat. "Sorry. You're right. So, did you and Cyrus...get along?"

"Not really."

He was delighted to hear it. "Why not?"

"He had some idea that a widow would tumble

into bed with the first man who asked, out of pure gratitude. He wasn't the least bit subtle about it, either. Halfway through the movie he suggested we leave and go back to his place so he could give me some relief from my frustration. I told him I'd rather see the end of the movie."

Sebastian smiled. Poor Cyrus, shot down by the Widow Lang. He loved it. "Must have been a good movie."

"Not very."

"Oh." Grinning wider, he glanced at the list again. "Well, I'd better get on over to your place, so I don't waste any more of the time Elizabeth's conked out. I'll be back as soon as I can make it. Feel free to help yourself to anything if you want a snack or something to drink."

"I always do."

"Yeah, that's the nice thing about being neighbors all these years." He backed toward the kitchen. "We're right at home in either house." And he wanted to keep it that way, which meant he'd better really know what he was doing if he decided to change things between them.

On his way to the back door, he glanced over at Fleafarm gazing expectantly at him from under the dining table. "Stay there, girl. Watch out for Matty and Elizabeth."

Fleafarm thumped her tail and put her head on her paws.

Sebastian grabbed his sheepskin coat and Stetson and headed out into the cold, dry air of a Colorado night.

Matty would have liked her book now instead of later. She needed to get her mind off the warmth of

Sebastian's hand on her arm, the look in his eyes when he'd stopped her from leaving the bedroom. She'd probably misinterpreted that look, but for a few seconds she'd thought he wanted to kiss her.

Well, he hadn't kissed her, so that probably meant she'd been wrong.

After glancing at Elizabeth to make sure she still slept, Matty wandered into the kitchen. She wasn't hungry or thirsty, but she needed something to do. But damned if she'd wash Sebastian and Charlotte's dinner dishes.

She prowled back into the living room and considered whether to build up the fire. Probably not. They'd all be going to bed soon.

To bed. She'd spent the night with Sebastian during roundup, but that had been in a crowd, not much intimacy involved. This didn't feel like roundup. And something about Sebastian was different tonight. Maybe it was second-hand desire courtesy of Charlotte.

Now that was enough to keep Matty riled for a good long while. She wasn't apt to do something stupid if she remembered that Sebastian was probably only giving off sexual vibrations that were leftover from Charlotte's visit. Unfortunately, that made perfect sense. If Sebastian had ever been interested in her body, he would have demonstrated his interest before tonight. It was no coincidence that his heated looks came a couple of hours after he'd been wrestling on the couch with Charlotte.

Sebastian wasn't the only one who was a bundle of frustrated hormones, Matty thought. Cyrus from the feed store had been partly right. She longed for a sexual relationship, but she was extremely picky about the person she had it with. In fact, she'd only considered one candidate, the man who was currently going over to pick up her undies. She wished she had some sexy ones.

With a sigh she turned toward the two cardboard boxes filled with Elizabeth's supplies. Maybe taking inventory and putting some of the items away would take her mind off that killer grin of Sebastian's when he'd discovered she hadn't wanted Cyrus's attentions. Male arrogance in all its glory. Sexy as hell. At that moment he'd been thinking that he could convince her to leave halfway through a movie. She could see it in his face. She couldn't let him know that with Sebastian, the pretense of going to a movie at all would be unnecessary.

Kneeling by the first box, Matty started pulling out terry sleepers, wash cloths and two hooded towels. At least the sleepers were all the same size, Matty noticed. Sleepers in graduated sizes would have been an alarming signal. But apparently Jessica expected to be back before the baby outgrew what was in the box.

Matty still couldn't imagine what would prompt a woman to leave her baby like this. Sebastian seemed to think Jessica was a wonderful person, but on the subject of women, he could be dense, as evidenced by his interest in Charlotte Crabtree of the manicured nails and salon-styled hair. Anyone with half a brain could see that Charlotte would never fit in with Sebastian's way of life. And Barbara had definitely been a bad choice.

Or maybe not. Both women had one thing that Matty didn't. They were both ultra-feminine, taking great pains to pamper themselves. On some level that must have appealed to Sebastian. They weren't common-sense women, either, which probably made him feel macho.

Taking a stack of sleepers, Matty stood and carried them into Sebastian's bedroom. Getting Elizabeth's clothes in there would go a long way to establishing where the baby would stay. Matty wasn't planning to be a glorified nanny, not even for Sebastian.

As she was laying the sleepers on top of the dresser, the phone rang. It made her jump and her heart pound faster until she realized it was probably Sebastian calling to ask about something on her list. Still, late-night phone calls gave her the creeps. She'd gotten the phone call about Butch's plane crash late at night.

She set down the sleepers and walked to the bedside table to pick up the receiver. "Forget something?"

"Uh, who is this?"

A female voice. God, did Sebastian have women stashed everywhere? If so, Matty decided it was time to record her own presence in his life. "I'm Matty Lang. Who are you?"

"Oh, *Matty.* Sebastian's neighbor. This is Jessica."

Matty almost dropped the receiver. "Where the hell are you? And what do you mean, leaving—"

"Matty, I had to." Her voice quivered. "It's killing me. Is she okay?"

"For now. But she needs you. Come back. I'm sure the problems can be worked out if you'll just—"

Click.

"Wait! Don't hang up!" Matty jiggled the disconnect button. "No! Come back on this line, dammit! I want to know if you..." The dial tone buzzed in her ear. "...if you slept with Sebastian," she finished softly. Then she replaced the receiver and stood staring at the rumpled sheets of his bed.

Sebastian might be dense about women, but he was the most honorable man Matty had ever met. She didn't believe that he was in love with Jessica, but if he'd fathered that baby, love wouldn't figure into it. He'd want to marry the mother of his baby. And Matty would lose him forever.

ON THE DRIVE over to Matty's, Sebastian couldn't stop thinking about her date with Cyrus. So she'd had a chance to go to bed with a virile young guy like Cyrus and had turned him down. Sebastian was immensely pleased that she'd done that, but he wondered if that only made the point that she wasn't very highly-sexed in the first place.

His first thought, and it was a dangerous one, was to accept that unspoken challenge. Where Cyrus had failed, Sebastian figured *he* could have convinced Matty to leave that movie, or whatever activity they were engaged in together. But what if he wasn't able to? What if she really wasn't very interested in sex?

It was definitely a case of damned if he did and damned if he didn't with Matty. And on top of everything else, there was the matter of Elizabeth. He had no business getting friendly with any woman until he found out for certain whether or not he was Elizabeth's father.

How ironic, that the moment he began thinking of getting back in the saddle, a baby would land on his doorstep, effectively putting him out of commission for the time being. Good thing Matty was the one staying in his house and helping him take care of the baby. Matty wasn't naturally seductive, so he should be able to keep his reactivated hormones in check.

Theoretically.

But once he was in Matty's bedroom going through her underwear drawer, breathing in her jasmine scent, he wasn't so sure he'd be able to keep his mind off lovemaking, after all. He couldn't understand why he was having this reaction to handling her panties and bra. They were exactly what he'd expect Matty to wear—cotton, plain and white. No frills. He was the kind of guy who appreciated black lace and dainty little bows in strategic places. These utilitarian items shouldn't have had any effect on him whatsoever.

Yet he stood in front of her dresser, rubbing the soft cotton between his fingers and feeling the first stirring of an erection. Maybe it was the basic nature of her underthings that appealed to some basic urge of his. Making love to Matty would be the real deal. No games, no artificial props. Instinctively he knew Matty would lay everything on the line when she climbed into bed with a man.

The idea shook him.

Beside him Sadie whined and thumped her tail on the floor.

"Time to get going, right, Sadie?" Thrusting inappropriate thoughts from his mind, Sebastian dropped the underwear in the bag along with a pair of wool socks. In the second drawer he found a pair of jeans. One more drawer down revealed a folded nightgown, right where she'd said it would be.

Underneath was a picture frame turned upside down. Feeling like a snoop, he took it out. Butch and

Matty's wedding picture. He vaguely remembered seeing it years ago.

Something wasn't right about the picture, and he finally realized it had been torn apart and taped back together. The taping job was good—he recognized Matty's care with detail. Someone had torn it down the middle lengthwise, separating the smiling bride in her simple white gown from the handsome groom in his western-styled black suit.

But they were back together now, wrapped in wedding-day bliss. Matty looked about sixteen, although he knew she'd been older than that when she'd married Butch—twenty-two or three. She looked breathtakingly beautiful, but it was the hopeful look in her eyes that made his heart ache. They'd been newlyweds when they'd moved onto the Leaning L ten years ago. Barely a year had gone by before Butch and Barbara had started their affair.

Sebastian gazed at the ripped picture and wondered whether Matty or Butch had torn it apart. Staring at Butch's cocky grin, Sebastian wished the son of a bitch was still alive so Sebastian could punch the smile right off his face. Not because of Barbara, who wasn't worth the effort of avenging, but because of Matty.

He had no doubt, looking at her expression in this picture, that she'd given herself heart and soul to Butch. Maybe she hadn't been as intensely passionate as a stud like Butch had required, but Sebastian would bet she'd given him all she had, and he'd paid her back with disloyalty. The ripped picture made Sebastian wonder if Matty had found that out.

Replacing the picture carefully the way he found it, he put the nightgown in the paper bag. It, too, was completely practical—a flannel granny gown with little sprigs of blue flowers forming the only decoration. The blue would go with her eyes, though. And if she wore nothing underneath, the gown suddenly became a lot less boring....

Sebastian let out a snort of self-disgust. Elizabeth was the important factor here, not his suddenly active sexual imagination. If he didn't hurry he'd be later than he'd promised getting back home.

Opening Matty's closet he took a long-sleeved shirt from its hanger, folded it and tucked it into the bag. Then he headed to the bathroom with Sadie trotting behind like a housebroken pony. A toothbrush, toothpaste, and a bottle of shampoo went into the bag.

The bottle of lotion took some effort. He had to screw the little pump handle into the neck of the bottle so the lotion wouldn't leak all over her clothes. In the process he got some on his hands. As he rubbed the cool, creamy stuff into his skin her jasmine scent wafted upward. Maybe this lotion was all she used to smell so wonderful.

He imagined her rubbing it all over herself after a shower. Then he imagined *helping* her rub it all over herself. With an impatient groan he dropped the bottle of lotion into the bag, picked it up and started for the front door, Sadie at his heels. He had his hand on the door knob before he remembered the book.

The book had been his idea, so she hadn't put it on the list, but now she'd expect it. Flipping on lights as he went, he retraced his steps to the bedroom with Sadie following along.

"I'll bet you think I'm an idiot," he said to the dog. "Well, you think right. If I'd had the guts to stay with that little baby, Matty would have come over to collect her belongings and I wouldn't have to be pawing through her underwear drawer. Serves me right for being such a coward."

Sadie made a little sound low in her throat and wagged her tail.

"I figured you'd agree with me." He walked over to the bedside table where a paperback lay with a bookmark stuck about a third of the way through. The cover featured a couple locked in a fevered embrace.

Sebastian had never thought much about what Matty read, but now out of curiosity, he picked up the book and opened it to the spot where she'd left off.

His eyes widened. "Whoa, Sadie." He flipped the page. "This is pretty hot stuff, dog. I'd go so far as to say X-rated." He read on until he realized his breathing was growing heavy right along with the hero's. Forcing himself to close the book, he dropped it in the bag.

Turning out lights once again and locking the front door carefully, he finally piled into his truck. Sadie sat regally in the passenger seat and Matty's bag of possessions rested in front of her on the floor.

"I sure wish you could talk," Sebastian said. "Because I thought I knew your mistress, but now I'm not so sure about that."

All the way back to the ranch he thought about that book she was reading. He was pretty sure that book offered a clue about the sort of lover Matty was, but he wasn't sure which clue.

On the one hand she could be the sort of woman who liked to think about lovemaking but didn't actually like doing it all that much. He'd heard about women like that.

On the other hand there was the possibility that she liked lovemaking very much, which was why she liked reading about it.

And the idea that she *might* be a tiger in bed was unsettling, to say the least. Because then he'd have to think about what it would be like to turn that tiger loose after all this time.

He'd better not think about that. Now was not the time to be setting any tigers loose. There might not ever be a good time for that, considering that they were neighbors and all.

As he pulled into the circular drive in front of the ranch house he decided he'd be wise to forget all about the book. And the panties. And the night-gown. And the lotion.

He let Sadie out and she frisked around him, nearly knocking him down as he reached in and got the bag. "You're gonna have to calm down," he warned the dog. "We have a baby in there, so you and Fleafarm have to mind your manners."

Sadie barked and bounded up the steps. From inside came an answering bark.

Matty opened the front door and grabbed Sadie's collar. "Easy does it, Sadie. Fleafarm, you stay back."

Sebastian looked at Matty standing in the doorway, the light from the living room surrounding her, seeming to make her glow. Exactly as he'd lectured himself not to, he thought about the book, and the panties, and the nightgown, and the lotion. He thought of Matty stretched out on rumpled sheets, Matty opening her arms, Matty drawing him close.

She met his gaze. It was probably his imagination, but he thought she quivered.

"Is everything okay?" he asked, his voice sounding a little rusty.

Her gaze didn't waver. "Jessica called."

6

Sebastian's hat brim partially shadowed his eyes, but Matty could still see well enough to judge whether Sebastian lit up when he heard Jessica had called. He'd said he didn't have a love affair going with her, but Matty still wanted a gut-check. The expression in those gray eyes reflected agitation, not agonized longing. Matty let out a breath. He wasn't in love with Jessica.

"Where is she?" Sebastian climbed the steps with the bag containing her clothes and toiletries in his arms.

"She didn't say." Still holding onto Sadie's collar with one hand and Fleafarm's with the other, Matty stepped back from the door to let him in.

He passed by her, trailing the scent of juniper and cold air. "Then why did she call?"

"To make sure Elizabeth was okay, I guess." Matty found this moment of homecoming way too appealing. It wasn't much of a stretch to imagine welcoming Sebastian home on a regular basis. "She was only on the line a few seconds. She asked if Elizabeth was okay, and I said she was."

"Did you tell her to get her butt back here?"

"I did. Listen, let me put these dogs in the kitchen where they can get reacquainted without waking up the baby."

"Good idea." Sebastian peered over toward the drawer. "Has she cried at all?"

"Not a peep. I think she's totally worn-out. We could probably detonate a bomb in here and she wouldn't wake up, but I don't want to push our luck."

"Hell, no." He gestured toward the kitchen. "There's a box of treats in the pantry if you want to bribe the dogs."

"I'd be happy to." She led the dogs into the other room. By the time she returned, closing the kitchen door after her, Sebastian had thrown his coat over the back of the sofa and laid his hat, brim up, on the coffee table. Matty's bag of belongings sat propped in the corner of the sofa and Sebastian was crouched down by Elizabeth's drawer-bed, gazing at the sleeping baby.

Matty would have liked some time to enjoy the picture of him studying the little girl, but at the click of the kitchen-door latch he looked over at her and stood.

"Did she say when she was coming back?" he asked.

"No. All she said was that she had to do this, and that it was killing her."

Sebastian frowned. "What in hell could be going on?"

"I don't know." Matty sat in the wing chair deliberately, so that Sebastian would have to take the rocker next to Elizabeth. A different sort of woman might have taken over the baby's care to make herself indispensable. Matty didn't operate that way. "What do you know about Jessica? Does she have family?"

He sat down carefully, glancing at the baby to make sure she didn't stir. "I gathered she's an only child and doesn't get along with her parents. They live back East somewhere, but she didn't like talking about her past."

"Do you think they abused her?"

"I honestly don't know." He gazed at Matty. "But there has to be some reason why she came here instead of going to them."

"She's had a baby out of wedlock. Lots of young women would hate telling their parents, especially if they didn't get along with them. Maybe she's leaving Elizabeth here while she goes back to prepare her folks." Yet even as she said that, Matty didn't believe it. "No, that's not the answer. She sounded too frantic about the baby's welfare when she called. If she only has to face a couple of disapproving parents, she'd have kept the baby with her."

"It's as if she's trying to protect Elizabeth from something."

Matty nodded. "While she tries to deal with it, whatever it is." She had a horrible thought. "I hope she doesn't have some terminal disease."

Sebastian sucked in a breath. "I hadn't even thought of that." He pushed himself from the chair and started to pace. "One thing's for sure, she doesn't want us looking for her, but I don't plan to abide by that."

"Are you going to call the cops?"

"No. Not until I know what we're dealing with. But my friend Jim can fix the phone so we can trace her calls, assuming she calls again."

"Is that legal?"

Sebastian gazed at her. "No. Gonna turn me in?"

"Of course not." Matty hesitated to ask the next question, but Sebastian needed to think of all the possibilities. "I know you consider Jessica a good friend, but you've only spent—what?—a total of five or six days with her?"

"Five, and I know that doesn't seem like enough time to judge a person, but sometimes time isn't everything. We've all made a joke about how Nat was completely buried in that avalanche, because I guess none of us want to think about how serious the whole thing was. If it hadn't been for Jessica's presence of mind, he probably would have died under that snow."

Matty's heart clutched. "I didn't realize it was that critical."

"It was. She saved his life."

"Then you don't think there's any possibility that she's...unbalanced."

"Nope. And I know she's cool under fire when she understands the problem. But she might have come up against something she doesn't know anything about, and maybe she's scared when she doesn't really need to be. That's why I'd like to quietly find her, to see if there's something I can do."

"I understand." In some ways, Matty never wanted Sebastian to find Jessica, because then he might discover that he was Elizabeth's father. But Matty knew that he wouldn't rest until he knew the truth.

"At first I'll try the easy stuff, like working with the phone. If that doesn't pay off, and she still hasn't turned up, I might consider a private investigator." He rubbed the back of his neck and gazed at the dying embers of the fire. "I don't suppose she mentioned anything about whether or not I was...."

"No."

"It's not the sort of thing you'd blurt over the phone. And Jessica isn't a coward, so she wouldn't announce it in the note she left with Elizabeth, either."

Matty grasped at whatever straw she could find. "Maybe you're not the father, and the real father is someone she doesn't want near Elizabeth."

Sebastian shook his head. "I can't see Jessica getting mixed up with anyone she wouldn't trust with the baby. She has too much self-confidence." He gazed at Matty. "I know this stunt she's pulled looks suspicious, but if ever I've met a woman whose head is screwed on straight, it's Jessica."

"Then I'm fresh out of explanations."

"Me, too. Something's got her spooked, that's for sure. If I am Elizabeth's father, I don't think she ever plans to tell me. I'll bet because I was drunk and didn't know what I was doing, she doesn't hold me responsible."

Feeling impatient, Matty pushed herself from the chair. "Then she doesn't know *you* very well, if she thinks you'd appreciate that kind of self-sacrificing gesture."

"True." He gazed down at the baby. "If she's mine, I intend to do right by her. And by her mother."

Matty's throat went dry. "Would you...marry her?"

He lifted his head and looked steadily at Matty. "If she'll have me."

She'd known all along that he'd feel that way, yet

hearing him say it was worse than imagining it might happen. "Even if you don't love her," she said woodenly.

"Yes, even then." He shifted his gaze to the fire and walked over to it. Moving the screen aside, he picked up the small fireplace shovel and started banking the ashes over the fiery coals.

Matty watched the play of muscles beneath his shirt as he worked and felt an agonizing tug of longing in the pit of her stomach. "And you're sure that's best?"

"I'm sure. My parents got a divorce when I was seven and my brother was five. For my folks, it was the best thing, because they fought like wildcats. It was probably best for my brother and me, too. We hated those fights they had." He cleared his throat and closed the damper part way. "But I would have given my right arm to have both a mom and dad around when I was growing up."

She'd never heard him admit that kind of vulnerability. The baby must be stirring up long-buried feelings from his childhood. She wanted to go over and put her arms around him, but that wouldn't be very appropriate considering he was telling her he was prepared to marry another woman.

"Your mom didn't remarry?" she asked.

"Not until I was out of the house." He replaced the screen and hung the shovel beside the hearth. "Which is just as well, because I don't get along with the guy." He shrugged, his back still to her, as if the discussion was easier on him that way. "My family's a disjointed mess. I've hated that rootless feeling, and no kid of mine will have that, if I have anything to say about it."

"But living with someone without loving them is hell."

Sebastian turned and shot her a questioning look.

Immediately Matty realized what she'd half revealed. "Or at least I imagine it could be." Her pulse raced as she wondered if he'd question her about that statement. She hoped he wouldn't, because she'd stopped loving Butch the day she found about the affair with Barbara. She and Butch had been fighting about whether Sebastian should be told the day Butch stormed off and slammed his plane into the mountain.

But it was all over now, and if Sebastian didn't know about Barbara and Butch, he didn't need to know. It would hurt him terribly to think he'd been betrayed by his good friend and his wife, and there was no point in dredging it up now that Butch was dead and Barbara was gone.

Indecision flickered in Sebastian's eyes, but in the end he glanced away as if willing to give Matty her privacy.

Her heartbeat slowed, and she took a long breath. In weak moments she wanted to pour the whole story out so that she and Sebastian could comfort each other. But it was a selfish urge, and she'd managed to curb it so far.

"I respect Jessica," he said quietly. "That could become a kind of love, and I'd work damn hard to try and make it happen. Maybe it wouldn't, but I can promise you we wouldn't fight the way my parents did."

"That sounds very noble, but I think children thrive better when their parents really love each other." She couldn't help herself. What he was proposing sounded like a living death. "My parents' marriage wasn't perfect—Dad depended way too much on Mom, which is why he's been such a basket case since she died. But one thing I'll carry with me forever is the picture of them walking down the street holding hands, or kissing each other just for the heck of it. You can't fake that kind of thing."

"I wouldn't fake it. If Jessica is the mother of my child, I'll teach myself to love her. And I'll teach her to love me."

Matty stifled a groan of despair. Knowing his iron will, he just might be able to do it. There was always the chance that Jessica wouldn't want such an arrangement, but Matty had a tough time imagining any red-blooded female resisting Sebastian if he poured his considerable resources into courting her. Yes, he might be able to teach himself to love the mother of his child. Now if only Matty could teach herself not to love Sebastian.

He gestured toward the paper sack. "I think it's all in there. Maybe we should try to get some sleep."

She nodded.

He started down the hall. "I'll make up the bed in the guest room for you."

"Just put the sheets in there," she said. "I'll put them on the bed. And I'll also keep the dogs in with me, too. All you need to do is carry that drawer into your room."

He turned with a half smile. "I thought maybe if I treated you real nice, like making up your bed and giving you the best towels, you'd take the drawer into your room."

"Nope."

He glanced uneasily toward the baby. "She's

probably going to wake up in the middle of the night, isn't she?"

"I think that's a good guess."

"Are you going to get up with me?"

"No, I'm going to let you do it all by yourself."

When he looked panic-stricken, she realized he didn't know she was kidding. "Yes, of course I'll get up with you," she said quickly. "Isn't that the whole point of having me stay overnight?"

"Then if you're getting up, too, why don't you just take her in with you? I'll be happy to keep Sadie and Fleafarm in my room."

"I'll bet you would. But that's not how we're doing this. I'll go see if the dogs want to go out before we close them in for the night." She started toward the kitchen.

"I know from being on roundup with you that I'm a much sounder sleeper than you are. What if I don't wake up when she starts crying?"

Matty chuckled. "That's why I want her right next to your bed instead of mine. After hearing the set of lungs on that kid, I have no doubt the person sharing a room with her will wake up. Even you. Just leave my sheets on the bed."

Sebastian heaved a dramatic sigh. "Okay."

WHEN THE FIRST wails came from the drawer beside his bed, Sebastian felt as if he hadn't slept at all, but a quick glance at the clock told him four hours had passed.

He switched on the light and fumbled for the jeans and T-shirt he'd left on the far side of the bed. Elizabeth's wails brought back the terror he'd felt when she'd first arrived, and he hurried into his clothes.

He needed to make that crying stop, both for her sake and his.

"Sebastian?" Matty rapped on his bedroom door. "Are you decent?"

"Yeah!" Relief flooded through him. Matty was awake. God bless her. He quickly zipped his jeans and reached for the T-shirt. By the time he'd pulled it over his head, Matty was crouched beside the drawer and reaching inside to take the wailing baby.

Groggy as he was, he couldn't miss how sweet she looked in that flannel granny gown, or how it flowed over her cute little butt when she leaned over. From her tousled blond hair to her sleep-pink cheeks, she looked exactly like the sort of woman a man dreamed of waking up to.

Even the buttoned-up neckline appealed to him. He'd been convinced that a woman needed scanty, sheer nightgowns to look sexy. He hadn't counted on the challenge to his manhood presented by a row of tiny buttons, or the lure of breasts demurely covered. When she stood up and cradled the baby in her arms, the weight pulled the material down so her breasts were outlined perfectly in soft blue and white cotton. His mouth watered.

Matty gave him a disparaging look. "I'm afraid upright isn't good enough. You're going to have to participate."

"Uh, right." Close call. She'd noticed his eyes glazing over and assumed sleepiness instead of arousal. He glanced away before she could reevaluate his expression. "What do you want me to do?"

"Go get her bottle ready while I change her. Then you can feed her."

Barefoot, he started toward the kitchen. "Where are the dogs?"

"I told them to stay in my room." She followed him down the hall. "They both went back to sleep."

"Lucky dogs." He turned on a lamp in the living room and continued on into the dining room.

"Don't you dare complain," Matty said. "I could be at home, you know, tucked into my warm bed, with at least an hour before the alarm went off."

"I know." He felt instantly contrite. "You're terrific to do this for me, Matty." He winced at the bright light as he flipped on the overhead in the dining room.

"We're neighbors," she said.

She said it so matter-of-factly that he was disappointed. "And friends," he added, looking at her.

"Yes, friends."

He gazed at her in the unflattering glare from the overhead light and couldn't get over how great she looked, how warm and cozy and inviting. He might have known Matty for ten years, but he realized now he'd never really seen her, at least not the way he was seeing her now.

He longed to stroke her smooth cheek. He wondered how that full lower lip would feel under the pad of his thumb, and if her eyes would darken if he rubbed his thumb back and forth over the moist surface.

"You're zoning out on me again," she said. "Snap out of it, Sebastian. Once you're settled in and feeding her, I'll make coffee. Until then you'll have to pull yourself up by your bootstraps. Honestly, I don't remember you being so loopy in the morning during roundup, even when you hadn't had your coffee." She positioned Elizabeth on the changing pad.

He thought about telling her what was making him loopy and discarded the idea. A man who might have to do the honorable thing before long didn't have a right to lust after his neighbor, who was only trying to be a friend. "Maybe I'm coming down with something," he said.

She glanced up at him. "Sounds like dishwasher's bellyache, to me. You're not getting out of this routine, Sebastian. Go fix her bottle."

"Yes, ma'am." He went into the kitchen, washed up and busied himself getting the bottle ready. He could hear Matty talking and crooning to Elizabeth, and the baby's cries became more sporadic. Even without experience, Matty was catching on fast. She was a born mother, he thought. Someday, somehow, she should have kids of her own.

Immediately desire stirred in him, restless and urgent. Damned if he knew why thinking of Matty as a mother should produce that sort of reaction. It sure as hell wasn't his job to take care of it. But the image of sinking into her flashed through his mind in vivid color and sound, like a tape that had been wound and ready, waiting for the proper cue. As he poured the formula his hands shook.

He had to take several deep breaths before his hand stopped trembling and he could finish getting the formula into the bottle. He tried to tell himself he was still stirred up from the episode with Charlotte, but that argument didn't wash. This wasn't about Charlotte, and he knew it. Charlotte hadn't inspired him to fantasize, not even after he'd kissed her. He hadn't even kissed Matty and his head was full of fantasies.

Perhaps they'd been trapped in his subconscious for years. If so, he wished he'd dusted them off a little earlier. Now was a very inconvenient time to develop a crush on his neighbor.

"Sebastian? You about finished?" Matty called. "She's almost ready for you."

"I'm on my way."

"Hurry up. I'm taking her into the living room."

"Okay." He smiled at the impatience in her voice. Making love to her would be a kick-and-a-half if she put even some of her normal spunk and sass into the endeavor. He had to stop thinking about the possibility, though.

But the minute he walked into the living room and saw her standing there, making love was all he could think about. Even the fretful baby in her arms didn't distract him.

Surely it was by accident that she'd placed herself in front of the lamplight as she stood near the rocking chair waiting for him. The light filtered through the nightgown, tracing her body underneath in loving detail. He stared, wetting dry lips.

Not that he didn't have a fair idea of her shape after seeing her in slim-cut jeans and tapered western shirts for the past ten years. But although her normal clothes defined her body, they acted almost like armor. Her loose nightgown was a flimsy, easily breached barrier between him and the naked woman underneath. She smiled and nearly gave him cardiac arrest.

"Quit stalling." Her voice was low and teasing. "And get over here."

A low, needy sound rumbled in his chest.

7

"SEBASTIAN?" MATTY FROWNED. He was standing there as if someone had hit him upside the head with a branding iron. Surely he wasn't this freaked out about feeding the baby. "Are you okay?"

He shook his head.

She melted. He *was* this freaked out. Scared speechless. She gentled her response. "Look, I can understand being scared the first time, but I got through it without killing her, and so can you. Let's forget about me making coffee for now. I'll stay with you and help you through this one time."

"It's...not the baby," he ground out.

"Not the baby?" That threw her. "Then what's wrong?"

"It's you."

"*Me?*"

"And that...that *nightgown*. And the way the light—" He waved a hand toward her in mute explanation.

When she finally understood what he was talking about, embarrassment hit her like a blast of superheated air. She glanced down reflexively but couldn't see what he was seeing from his vantage point. Stepping away from the lamp, she clutched the baby closer to her chest.

Mortification clogged her speech. "I...didn't realize I was displaying myself. Sorry." Oh, God. She prayed he wouldn't think she'd done that on purpose.

Elizabeth fussed and wriggled in her arms, and Matty loosened her death grip on the baby.

"Matty, you—"

"Sit in the rocker, Sebastian." She avoided his gaze but hadn't missed the bulge in his jeans. How nice if that reaction was for her, but she knew better. He wasn't turned on by her, not dressed in her conservative little granny gown. He was still revved up from his bout with Charlotte, and the shadow of her naked body had reminded him of unsatisfied needs. "We have to get this baby fed."

He walked over and eased into the rocker, the bottle in his right hand.

Matty's breathing was uneven as she leaned over him and settled Elizabeth in the crook of his left arm. His warmth and the scent of aroused male nearly caused her to moan aloud. None of it was because of her, she reminded herself again. "Now offer her the...nipple," she said in a ragged voice.

The bottle trembled in his grip. It took a couple of tries before Elizabeth connected. At last she grabbed on and started to suck.

Matty backed off, her pulse racing. "Got her?"

"I guess." He focused on the baby, but his voice was hoarse, as if he hadn't put sexual thoughts completely behind him. "Is that angle right, or should I prop her up more?"

"That looks about right." She backed away from the rocker and crossed her arms over her chest. "Um, do you have a bathrobe I can borrow? I should have asked you to bring mine, but I didn't think of it."

He gazed up at her. "Listen, don't—"

"Or maybe I should just get dressed. That might be the best thing."

"Please don't leave me here alone with this baby so you can cover yourself up."

She swallowed. "I feel uncomfortable."

"You're not in the light now. It's okay."

Her cheeks still felt very warm. "I don't want you ever to think that I would deliberately...." She couldn't bring herself to spell out what she would never, ever do, but she figured he'd understand the unspoken thought.

"You think I don't know that about you? That's what made the moment so...effective. You didn't mean to. You were just...there."

She swallowed again and looked up at the ceiling. If only she could believe he was really attracted to her. But she couldn't, and so his words made her feel lonesome and teary-eyed. "I suppose you were pretty frustrated when the baby arrived in the middle of your evening. Any old body probably would turn you on about now."

His voice was soft. "I don't think so, Matty."

She didn't want him deluding either himself or her. She brought her gaze back to his. "Oh, come on, Sebastian. I've been your neighbor for ten years. If the sight of me turned you on, you'd have figured that out a long time ago."

"You'd think so, wouldn't you?" He looked confused. And oh, so sexy, in his T-shirt and jeans, his hair mussed and stubble shadowing his jaw. And to top it all off, he was holding a pink confection of a little baby cuddled against his chest.

Matty fought the urge to take what she could get

from him, second-hand though it might be. But the reckoning would come eventually, and she'd hurt less if she stayed strong now. "The explanation's pretty obvious. You're reacting to this whole situation—Charlotte, the baby, Jessica, the possibility that you're a father. Your libido's waking up, and I happen to be handy."

He gazed at her, the heat still simmering in his eyes. "Are you trying to convince you or me?"

She sighed and looked away from that heat. A girl could only take so much temptation. "Maybe both of us. I don't want to be caught in a hail of hormones."

"And that's the only reason I feel like kissing you right now? I'm being pelted with hormones?"

Her pulse rate shot up a few more notches and her lips began to tingle. She didn't dare look at him or she'd stare at his mouth and imagine...everything. "Have you ever felt like kissing me before?"

"Yeah."

If he confessed to an obsession he'd carried around for years, then she might change her mind about things. "When?"

"Last night."

Her one tiny hope died. "That doesn't count. You were already in the middle of this thing by then. I mean before that."

"Not that I remember," he said with blunt honesty.

She fought back disappointment. She had to be sensible about this, or her heart would be broken beyond repair. "That makes my point. It's not me. It's the situation. Can I borrow your bathrobe?"

"Don't have one."

"Then I'll get dressed." As she started out of the

room, Elizabeth began to choke. Matty spun around and hurried back to him.

He'd already jerked the bottle from her mouth and set it on the table beside him, but he was frozen, obviously unsure what to do next. "Do something!" he cried.

"Put her up to your shoulder and pat her back," Matty instructed.

He scooped her up awkwardly and propped her against his shoulder while she sputtered. "She's still choking! What if she dies?"

"She won't." Even though Matty had refused to assume full care of her nieces and nephews at this age, she'd been around them enough to know this little sputtering wasn't dangerous. "She just got a little down the wrong drain. Pat her."

He patted. "It's not working!"

"Like this." Matty leaned over him, grasping the arm of the rocker for balance as she tapped her palm against the baby's back.

Gradually Elizabeth's sputters subsided. She coughed a couple of times and relaxed against Sebastian's shoulder.

"There," Matty said with relief. She started to lever herself away.

"Matty." He'd never said her name quite that way before, low and rich with meaning.

Her breath caught. Slowly she turned her head and looked into his warm, compelling eyes. His beautiful mouth was inches from hers.

"Matty." A plea. A plea that was reflected in his eyes.

"You don't want me," she whispered.

He didn't answer, just gazed at her with that heart-stopping expression in his eyes.

She lost the battle. With a soft moan she leaned closer...and slowly touched her lips to his.

He met her halfway, molding his mouth against hers in gentle welcome.

At the heady contact, she grew dizzy. She'd dreamed this moment so many times...perhaps she was dreaming still. Ah, but his sculpted lips felt good against hers, and the contact made there, mouth against mouth, echoed all the way to her toes.

Breathless from the richness of it, she drew back. Struggling to compose herself, she gazed at him and wondered if he'd disappear in the fog of yet another dream.

But he was right there, solid and real, his eyes still closed. "That...was so sweet," he whispered.

"I shouldn't have."

Slowly his eyes opened and his voice was a gentle murmur. "*We* shouldn't have," he corrected. "But it felt damn good."

"Too good." She wanted to kiss him again. From the warm glow in his eyes, he wanted that, too. Summoning all her strength, she stood and backed away from the chair. "You'd better finish feeding her."

His gaze traveled over her nightgown, lingering where her aroused nipples pushed against the flannel. Finally he looked up into her eyes. "We've always been able to talk to each other, Matty. We should be able to talk about this."

She didn't want to talk. She wanted to make love to him, as unwise as that might be. But he wasn't suggesting that. He was suggesting conversation.

"I can talk better with my clothes on," she said.

"Let me hook her up with the bottle before you leave, just so I know she's not going to start choking again." His movements were tentative, but he managed to position Elizabeth approximately the way she'd been lying before. Picking up the bottle, he offered it to the baby. She took the nipple eagerly, patting the bottle with both hands as she stared up at Sebastian.

Matty's heart wrenched at the touching picture they made—Sebastian with his beard-shadowed jaw and Elizabeth with her baby-smooth skin. Touching and ultimately frustrating. He was everything Matty had ever wanted. And that sweet-faced baby in his arms might be the one thing that would keep her from having her chance with him.

OPPORTUNITIES to talk about that all-important kiss were in short supply, Sebastian realized later. By the time he finished giving Elizabeth her bottle Matty was dressed, had let the dogs out for a run and had coffee brewing. She'd also fixed her hair into a single golden braid, and he suspected she'd done it on purpose, as if taming her hair would tame her impulses.

While he grabbed a quick shave and shower, Matty changed the baby. He dressed quickly and found them both in the kitchen, Elizabeth perched in her infant seat on the kitchen counter and Matty hauling out a frying pan, eggs and bacon. The picture made his heart squeeze. He hadn't realized how much he'd longed for a family scene like this one. Unfortunately it was an illusion.

And because it was, he couldn't impose on Matty to cook for him. "Let me do that." He moved to take the frying pan from her hand.

She lifted it out of reach. "You need to go feed your animals." Setting the pan on the stove, she turned around and poured coffee into a mug. "Take some coffee with you. I know how you get without caffeine." She held the mug toward him. "I'll fix breakfast while you're out in the barn."

The coffee smelled terrific and he took it with gratitude. He lifted the mug in salute. "Thanks." He took a swallow and sighed with satisfaction. "Good coffee."

"Glad you like it." With a faint smile she turned back to the stove and opened the package of bacon.

He liked more than the coffee. He liked the way her jeans fit smoothly over her butt. Tough to believe he'd never taken the time to admire that before. "Really," he said. "Don't worry about fixing breakfast. I'll do it when I get back in." He was used to Barbara, a reluctant riser who had left the coffee and breakfast preparations to him.

She continued laying slices of bacon in the pan. "And what am I supposed to do in the meantime, twiddle my thumbs?"

Barbara would never have asked a question like that, he thought. She had always jumped at the chance to dodge a chore. "Just relax. Read a book or something."

"You mean the baby book Jessica sent?"

"No, I meant the one I brought over here last night." Then he remembered the hot scene where her bookmark had been, which reminded him of their kiss, and he wanted to forget about coffee, forget about feeding his animals, forget about breakfast.

"I'm not on vacation, Sebastian." She finished arranging the slices and wiped her hands on a paper towel. "Besides, we need to get going. After we take care of things at my place, I think we should make a run into town and look for a changing table and maybe a crib."

He didn't want to go to town. Outside the kitchen window he could see a storm threatening. Gray clouds hung over the mountains and the wind was kicking up. He wanted to light the fire and cuddle with Matty, which was, of course, the last thing he should be considering.

From her infant seat, Elizabeth made a gurgling noise, drawing his attention. She seemed to be looking at him. She jammed her hand in her mouth, pulled it out again, and gurgled again.

The nose, he thought. That could definitely be a Daniels' nose on that baby. "She seems happy," he said.

Matty turned the burner on low under the bacon and glanced over at Elizabeth. "I think she's doing okay."

He took a sip of his coffee. "Do you suppose she misses Jessica?"

"Probably. At least she's young and adaptable."

His gut clenched. "You say that as if she'll never see her mother again. Jessica will be back in a few days."

The bacon began to sizzle in the pan and Matty turned it with a fork. "Then why did she leave instructions on what immunizations she should have at four months?"

"*What?*"

Matty glanced at him. "I skimmed through the whole set of instructions while you were in the shower. At the end is the immunization schedule. It goes up through fifteen months.''

FIFTEEN MONTHS. Sebastian thought about that as he doled out hay and made sure the watering troughs in each stall were working. Fleafarm led Sadie through the barn as if giving a tour. His dog loved company, Sebastian thought. He should have kept one of her pups, but Barbara had been dead set against it.

Sebastian was only now beginning to realize how rigid and demanding Barbara had been, and that most women didn't behave that way. His mother was a lot like Barbara, so he'd been programmed to accept that kind of behavior. But after having Matty in the house less than twenty-four hours, he could appreciate the benefits of having a willing partner.

A willing partner. Now there was a phrase with a sexy ring to it. Of course, he did seem to have sex on the brain at the moment. In fact, he couldn't remember the last time he'd been this frustrated and confused about life in general.

Good thing he had this chance to work in the barn. The scent of horsehide and saddle leather and the presence of his animals always calmed him in times of stress. And that kiss, paired up with the recently unearthed immunization schedule for Elizabeth had provided a fair amount of stress.

Well, this little caper wouldn't go on for fifteen months, and that was all there was to it. He wasn't about to wait that long to find out whether he was the father of the little munchkin making goo-goo eyes in his kitchen.

Because if he wasn't Elizabeth's father, then

maybe, just maybe, he would consider exploring this crazy new thing with Matty. Discovering his attraction to her after all these years had knocked him off his pins, and he still wasn't sure what to do about it. He thought she might be interested in him, too. That kiss had aroused her, at least.

Still, she'd talked a lot about how he'd been carried away by the circumstances they found themselves in. He didn't think that was true for him, but maybe she was trying to tell him she had been carried away. She wouldn't want them to louse up their neighborly cooperation any more than he would. A love affair had the potential to do that.

It also had the potential to transform their lives into something spectacular.

It could go either way, and he'd question the wisdom of courting Matty even if the baby hadn't shown up. The baby, however, made courting Matty the dumbest idea in the world. Of course, if it hadn't been for the baby he might never have seen Matty in a different light. Literally.

He finished up in the barn, whistled for the dogs and started back up toward the house. He'd always been proud of the log house with its stone fireplace, relaxed design and generously-sized windows.

Those windows gave him a million-dollar view of the Sangre de Cristo Mountains and he'd framed the view by planting aspens on either side of the front porch. The branches were bare now, but soon after his birthday they'd be bursting with tender green leaves. He loved springtime.

Returning to the house he'd built used to give him great pleasure when his marriage was new and all things seemed possible. The pleasure had eluded him in the past few years, but he felt its tug again this morning, and he didn't have to look very hard for the reason. Matty was inside, waiting for him.

As the dogs pranced around him, the wind pulling at his hat smelled like rain, or maybe even snow. He wondered if it was a good idea to take a little baby out in that kind of weather. Yet going into town would be a distraction and give them some distance from that kiss.

They should probably do it. If the storm hit later today then the roads would get bad, and they might not have another chance this week to get the baby furniture. Not that he wanted baby furniture. It made the whole setup look way too permanent. He wouldn't even mind that so much, if he just knew whether or not he was Elizabeth's daddy.

He was not a man who enjoyed uncertainty.

8

FROM THE KITCHEN WINDOW Matty had a view of the path down to the barn, and when she saw Sebastian close the barn door and start toward the house, she cracked the eggs into the pan. Bacon and hash browns were staying warm in the oven and bread perched in the toaster.

She'd spent plenty of time in this kitchen when Barbara was still around, so she knew where everything was kept. Barbara had barely tolerated having to cook and had been eager for Matty's help whenever Matty and Butch had come over for dinner.

Matty didn't consider herself particularly domestic, either. She always preferred to be outside working with her animals than inside fussing over a stove or a mop bucket. But household help didn't come cheap, so she did the work and found no value in complaining about it.

Even so, this was more effort than she'd put into a meal in years. And the reason was striding up the hillside toward her, head bowed against the wind, the collar of his sheepskin coat turned up to block out the chill.

She took this opportunity when he wouldn't catch her to admire his awesome physique—strong legs that could grip a bucking horse or lead his partner through a country waltz, powerful arms that could lift an orphaned calf onto his saddle or comfort a grief-stricken young widow. Just looking at him elevated her blood pressure.

He liked his eggs over easy. Not crinkled and hard around the edges, although he'd eat them that way, and not hard-cooked, although he'd eat them that way, too. Sebastian never complained about the food someone served him, but Matty happened to know his preference was over easy and moist in the middle. She wondered if he liked his women that way. If so, she'd fit the bill.

The trick to over-easy eggs was keeping the temperature low. She slid the spatula under the eggs to make sure they weren't sticking to the bottom of the cast-iron skillet. So far, so good.

From her infant seat propped on the counter, Elizabeth began to fuss.

"Not now, baby," Matty crooned, watching the egg whites slowly grow opaque. Patience was everything when you were going for over easy.

Elizabeth started to cry.

Matty glanced at the baby, but couldn't see anything wrong with her. Shoot. If she left the eggs they'd be ruined. She scoured her memory, trying to remember what her sister used to do to distract a crying kid.

Pris used to sing to her babies, nice little lullabies or perky tunes about cats and rabbits. Matty couldn't carry a tune in a bucket, although she obviously had to do something. And she didn't know any kiddy songs, either. But she knew Alan Jackson's *Chattahoochee*.

So she started singing to Elizabeth about muddy water and beer cans in the moonlight. Elizabeth kept on crying, so Matty got louder as she popped the lever down on the toaster.

When louder didn't seem to cut it, Matty started to dance. Spatula in hand, she wiggled, kicked and stomped, flipping the eggs when the time was absolutely, perfectly right. If she had anything to say about it, these eggs were going to be primo.

When Elizabeth stopped crying, Matty looked over and saw the baby watching her with round eyes. She grinned and added a couple of flourishes. She'd loved line dancing to this tune back in the days when she did such things, a million years ago.

Because the dance steps were grooved into her memory, she didn't have to concentrate on them and could focus on the eggs. There. Exactly right. She flipped the over-easy eggs onto a plate, stomping her feet in time to her singing. A moist-cooked egg had shimmy to it. These two babies shimmied beautifully.

With a cocky little grapevine step she sashayed over to the oven and swung her bottom in time to the rhythm while she dished bacon and hash browns around the outstanding eggs.

When the plate was loaded, she spun in time to the music...and came face-to-face with a grinning Sebastian.

She dropped the plate.

Swearing took the place of singing as she stared at the mess on the floor. Both dogs rushed forward. "Stay!" she ordered, pointing at them.

"I'll put them outside until we get this cleaned up." He shooed the dogs out the door while Matty brought the garbage pail over and then dug in the cupboard under the sink for a bucket and sponge.

"I'm sorry I startled you," Sebastian said.

"Those eggs were *perfect*," she wailed, scooping broken crockery and scattered hash browns into the garbage.

"The line dance was better." His voice was rich with laughter and male appreciation as he crouched down to help. "I can have eggs any day."

"Not like this, you can't." She swiped up egg yolk with the sponge and waggled it under his noise. "Over easy and moist in the middle. They were masterpieces."

God, she was wonderful, Sebastian thought as he dropped another piece of broken plate in the garbage. He'd seen enough of her performance to know that nothing that exciting had ever gone on in this kitchen. Many an evening he'd shared the same dance floor with Matty, but he'd been with Barbara, and she'd been with Butch. He hadn't let himself notice the tempting wiggle of her bottom.

Elizabeth started crying, and he glanced up at the infant seat on the counter. "What's with the munchkin?"

"Don't know. She wouldn't be hungry this soon. I checked the schedule." She kept mopping. "I found out that dancing makes her stop crying. Wanna take a turn?"

He chuckled. "Only if you'll sing."

"I can't sing."

"Sure you can. You're just terrible at it."

She glanced at him. "Are you insulting my singing?"

The floor was a mess, the baby was crying, and all he could think about was kissing her. Wisps of golden hair had escaped her prim braid to curl around her flushed face. Her blue eyes were bright with challenge...and something more potent than that.

Her breath hitched, as if she could read the message in his eyes loud and clear. "Because if you're going to insult my singing, then you get to pick up the baby and find out if she has a poopy diaper, which I think might be her problem."

She knew how to puncture a mood, all right. "Hey, you might sing bad, but you're top-notch at that dancing thing."

"Too late." She returned to her cleaning. "You can't sweet-talk your way out of it, now, cowboy. You're on diaper duty."

He grimaced and stood, knowing he might as well face this chore now as later. Going over to the sink, he washed his hands, hoping maybe Elizabeth would stop crying while he was doing that. She didn't.

"While you're changing her, I'll make some more eggs."

"We could have cereal instead."

"No, I have my mouth set for eggs, and the bacon and hash browns are already made."

"Then let me make them," he suggested hopefully. "You probably don't want to go through all that again."

"As opposed to changing a dirty diaper?" She looked up at him and grinned. "I may not know much about this baby business, but I know which areas to stay away from."

AN HOUR LATER they'd left the dogs to watch the place, belted Elizabeth's seat into the back of Sebas-

tian's Bronco, and set off for Matty's. By the time
they pulled up in front of the barn at the Leaning L,
Elizabeth had dozed off. They had a low-pitched but
heated discussion about who would stay with the
baby and who would feed Matty's horses. Matty
won.

She wasn't a traditional female, Sebastian thought
as he watched her hurry into the barn. She'd never
be content to tend to household duties and let the
men handle the ranch work. Barbara hadn't been traditional, either, but in a different way. She hadn't
been interested in housekeeping, but unfortunately
she hadn't liked ranch work any better. Once she'd
discovered how much physical exertion was involved, she'd started yearning for a desk job.

Now she had one, although she was seldom behind her desk. As a travel agent she had an excuse to
go all over the place. He often wondered if the post-
cards she sent were her way of thumbing her nose at
his willingness to be tied down to a piece of land and
a bunch of critters.

Matty understood that in him. In fact, there wasn't
much about him that Matty didn't understand. She
even knew exactly how he liked his eggs. She must
have been paying pretty close attention over the
years to pick up on that. Of course Matty had always
been sensitive to people's likes and dislikes, but Sebastian wondered if there was more to it. He liked
the idea that there *was* more to it.

And that made him a heel, because if Matty had a
crush on him he couldn't do a damn thing about it
right now. And he needed to discuss that with her,
somehow. She'd kissed him, and he'd kissed her
back. They couldn't pretend that nothing had

changed. But it couldn't keep changing in that direction.

As he sat waiting for Matty, he glanced around, taking inventory of the Leaning L in a way he seldom had the leisure to do. The barn was in pretty good repair, which didn't surprise him considering Matty's priorities. She'd want her animals housed in more splendor than herself, if it came to a choice. Obviously she didn't have time to maintain both buildings in top condition.

Travis did all he could for her in the summer months, but Travis had his own place in Utah and he left every fall once the summer cattle were rounded up and shipped to market. Even from this distance Sebastian could tell the ranch house needed a coat of paint.

He'd never cared much for the style of the frame-and-stucco house, which looked like it belonged in California, in Sebastian's estimation, with its white exterior and red-tiled roof. Butch had loved the look, loved the idea of standing out against the mountains, meadows and forest.

The passenger door opened and Matty slipped inside, closing the door gently. She plopped a small satchel on the floor. "I've been thinking of painting the house beige," she said, as if reading his mind.

"When?"

"That's just it." She fastened her seat belt. "I have time in the winter but it's too cold. In the summer I have no time."

"I didn't know you wanted to paint it." He put the Bronco in gear and started down her lane. "We could round up some neighbors this summer and get it done."

"Oh, Sebastian, I hate the idea of corralling everybody to help out the poor Widow Lang. I've always—"

"For God's sake, Matty." He found himself angrier than he should have been. Maybe he was ticked at himself for not noticing that she needed more help than he'd been giving. "It wouldn't kill you to accept a gesture like that. People enjoy the sense of community they get from it. Damn, but you're a proud woman. Too proud for your own good."

She took the comment in silence, and instantly he felt sorry for blasting her like that. "Okay, if you have to do something in return, you could dance for us while we painted." He glanced over at her to see if that made her smile.

It did. "I'd rather sing for y'all," she said, a twinkle in her eye.

"I think we'd all be grateful if you'd dance, instead."

"I could do both."

"You could, but I doubt anybody would get any painting done, what with falling off the ladders laughing our asses off."

Matty smiled and leaned her head back against the seat. "I *would* like to get the place painted. I've always hated the stark white. Sticks out like a sore thumb. I like the way your house blends into the landscape."

"After you and Butch built your house, Barbara wanted me to paint ours white."

Her head came up and she stared at him. "Yuck! Paint those beautiful logs white? What was she thinking?"

"That we blended in too much."

Matty rolled her eyes. Then she grew thoughtful. "They were a lot alike, Butch and Barbara."

"Guess so." He kept his tone casual, but he was instantly on the alert to see if anything about her manner would indicate that she'd known about the affair.

She gave nothing away. "Must be true, that opposites attract," she said.

"At least when you're young. Somebody different from you seems more exciting." At the moment he couldn't think of anyone more exciting than Matty performing her little line dance in his kitchen. If there had been no baby, and no other considerations, he could easily have made love to her right there on the kitchen floor.

"We were young, all right," Matty said. "All four of us, just starting out, determined to make a go of it."

Sebastian smiled grimly. "Some of us more than others."

"Yeah." She gazed out at the cloud-covered mountains. "Once Butch bought that plane, he didn't have much interest in ranch work. Remember how he claimed he'd use it to spot cattle, and even herd them with it?"

"Yep. And he never got around to it."

"Too busy making little trips here and there to ever try using it for cattle control."

Sebastian had learned from Barbara that Butch's trips had been coordinated with her shopping jaunts to the big city. He and Matty must have been blind as bats not to put it all together. Then again, maybe she had, which would explain the torn picture.

"What do you plan to tell people?" Matty asked.

"About what?" For one wild moment he thought she was talking about Butch and Barbara.

"Elizabeth. We'll have her with us, and we'll be buying baby furniture. We'll cause a stir. What do you want to say?"

He'd never considered the problem. But no question, it *was* a problem. They needed the baby furniture. After the wrestling match he'd had with Elizabeth while changing her diaper this morning he agreed with Matty that they needed a changing table he could strap the kid to, at the very least. A crib would be nice, too. He'd found a sliver in the drawer, and he didn't want to take any chances Elizabeth would hurt herself.

But he couldn't pop into town with a baby without starting seventeen kinds of gossip. That is, if Charlotte hadn't started it already. He'd better figure out which direction he wanted to channel that gossip.

"You're a lousy liar, by the way," Matty added helpfully.

"Then I guess I don't have much choice of what to say, do I? The truth is all I can manage."

"Well, you don't have to tell the *whole* truth, and if Jessica is in some sort of trouble, you don't want to make things worse for her."

Sebastian chuckled. "Let me take a guess. You've worked this all out, haven't you?"

"Somebody had to, and it's obvious it wasn't going to be you."

He got such a kick out of her. She could cram more thinking into ten minutes than he could accomplish in ten hours. "You might as well tell me what to say and get it over with, Matty."

"Okay, here's how you phrase it. *I'm taking care of*

this baby for a friend who needs a little space right now. Matty's helping me. And then you shut up. Don't add anything, or you'll get yourself in trouble."

"Do you think they'll wonder if the baby's mine?"

"Of course. Don't confirm or deny, as they say in politics. You can't stop them from speculating. After all, that's one of the main activities in Huerfano."

"Maybe they'll look at her and see a resemblance."

"Do you see a resemblance?"

"I don't know. Sometimes I think I do. Her nose, maybe."

"Her *nose?*"

"Yeah." Sebastian couldn't decide if he wanted to find family traits in Elizabeth or not. On the one hand he didn't want to think he'd been irresponsible, and despite what he'd said about making himself love Jessica, he didn't think that was the best way to approach marriage. On the other hand he'd always wanted a kid. So he kept looking, to see if he now had one. "Her nose looks like a Daniels' nose."

"Then you must be thinking of a stray branch in your family tree, because her nose is nothing like yours. You have a strong nose, sort of like the profile of those Roman emperors. Elizabeth's nose tips up. It's cute, not strong."

"She's little. It could get stronger."

"But that tilt at the end's not going to go away. If you're basing this on her nose, I think you're off base."

"Well, her eyes, then."

"They look as much like mine as yours."

He blew out an impatient breath. "Doggone Jessica for not telling me, one way or the other. Especially considering..." He paused, not sure how to get into the subject of him and Matty.

"Considering you're starting to date again?" Matty suggested gently.

Funny how ever since he'd kissed Matty, the idea of dating had lost all appeal. He decided he couldn't lead up to this. He'd have to jump in headfirst. "I really liked kissing you, Matty." He kept his gaze fixed on the road.

"I liked kissing you, too, Sebastian."

"And even if you kissed me, I was the one who started it, and I accept the responsibility for it."

Matty sighed. "Sebastian, I think you'd accept the responsibility for the sun coming up every morning if somebody hinted that you should. But we're going to share the responsibility for that kiss. I knew it was probably a big mistake. Nobody held a gun to my head."

"What if it wasn't a mistake?" Sebastian asked softly, and risked glancing over at her. "If Elizabeth didn't figure in, that is."

Her cheeks grew pink. "It was. Even if Elizabeth didn't exist."

"But—"

She held up her hand. "I've worked it out."

"I'll just bet you have," he muttered.

"After Barbara left, you shut down for a while, which makes perfect sense. But now you've decided to become involved with women, again. And all those needs you've been suppressing are bubbling to the surface. Suddenly good old Matty, who never appealed to you sexually before, seems like the best thing since sliced bread. Once you got that out of your system, I'd go back to being good old Matty—a nice person, but not someone who turns you on."

"You think that's the kind of fickle person I am?"

"Not naturally, but you've been through some rough times, and I think your radar's off."

"Or it's finally starting to work right." He wouldn't hurt Matty for the world, but he didn't think she had this as nailed down as she thought. "And what about you? You could be attracted to me for the same reasons, and don't tell me you're not attracted, because I know different."

"Of course I'm attracted," she said softly.

Just like that, he was aroused. He wanted to pull the Bronco off to the side of the road and reach for her. But there was a baby in the back seat. "We might have something, here, Matty. No matter what you say, we just might. And what kills me is that we can't do anything about it, because first I have to find out what Jessica has to say."

She turned toward him, her shoulder pulling against the seat belt. "And that's where you and I disagree. I think it would be a mistake for us to get involved, but not because of the baby." Her blue gaze sharpened. "You deserve to marry for love, Sebastian, not convenience, or some overblown sense of loyalty. If you're Elizabeth's father, you can still be a devoted parent without the sacrifice of shackling yourself to a woman you don't love."

A band of tension made his hat feel a size too tight. "That baby didn't ask to be born. Her welfare is my top priority."

"That may be a good thing, because it'll keep you from doing something foolish with your neighbor."

He thought about spending at least another night

with Matty and groaned. "Maybe I should hire that nurse you talked about."

"If you want."

"I don't. I want you to help me, Matty. I'll just have to keep my mind off of...what I've been thinking about."

She lifted the satchel she'd brought. "I picked up my bathrobe."

"That'll help."

"Let me know if there's anything else."

He glanced at her, taking in her pink, kissable lips, her soft blue eyes, her golden hair. She'd have a hell of a time taking care of Elizabeth with a bag over her head. "Don't dance," he said.

9

WHEN MATTY USED HER HEAD, she believed everything she'd told Sebastian. But her heart wanted to argue. Her heart dreamed about a fairy-tale ending in which Sebastian had finally discovered that Matty was the woman for him. If he'd admitted to ever having yearned for her in the past ten years, she might be more willing to listen to her heart.

But no. He claimed to have had his first arousing thought about her the night before. That was a little too coincidental for Matty's tastes.

She was relieved when they pulled up in front of Huerfano's only department store. Being confined in the Bronco with Sebastian, who seemed about to swear that he suddenly lusted after her body, was plain uncomfortable.

She glanced over a couple of spaces and recognized Gwen Hawthorne's violet truck parked in front of the store. "Gwen's here," she said with pleasure. "I'll bet she's picking up yarn for a new project." Gwen owned a bed-and-breakfast outside of town, and she and Matty shared a passion for weaving that had evolved into a close friendship.

"I don't know if that's so good, her being here." Sebastian turned off the engine. "I was hoping we could try out our story on somebody we don't know as well. Gwen's not going to be satisfied with that bare-bones version you want me to hand out."

"She will if we ask her to be, for now. Elizabeth won't be a mystery baby forever, and once we know the truth, Gwen can be the first one we tell."

"If you say so." He opened the door, and cold air whipped in the cab. He closed the door again and glanced at her. "Want to handle it with Gwen?"

She could see he'd bungle the explanation, which would make life more difficult for them if people started calling the ranch or worse, driving out to catch a glimpse of Elizabeth. "Okay, I'll do the talking."

He let out a breath. "Thanks. I wasn't—"

"But I think you should carry Elizabeth."

"Oh." He got that scared-little-boy look that made her want to hug him.

"You'll be fine," she said. "You've been carrying her in the house."

"Yeah, but now we'll be in a store. Stuff is closer together. I could turn wrong and bang her head against a shelf, or stumble over something and both of us could go down, and if I landed on top of her, I'd crush her like a pop can."

The image made Matty wince, but Sebastian needed to get used to hauling Elizabeth around. Matty wasn't willing to hang around the Rocking D until Jessica showed up. "Take it slow, and you'll be fine."

"She's still asleep. How about if I stay here and you go in? Just pick out what you want, and then come back out and I'll go in and pay for it, and load it in the back."

"I'm not buying this furniture without you. And

besides—'' She turned as Elizabeth started fussing from the back seat. ''Besides, she's awake. Come on. Let's get this accomplished so we can get home. I want to read that section in the book on baths. We should probably give her one.''

''Oh, Lord. A bath.''

''And she'll be hungry soon.''

Sebastian stared at her. ''I just thought of something. Should we have brought stuff like a bottle and diapers?''

Matty stared back at him, and slowly she remembered how her sister used to go out laden down with everything but the kitchen sink, even for a short trip. ''I never thought.''

''Let's get this show on the road.'' Sebastian looked like a man approaching the hangman's noose, but he got out of the Bronco and headed for the back seat and Elizabeth.

Matty helped him extricate the little girl from her seat and shield her from the bitter wind as they hurried into Coogan's Department Store, a place that would have been called Coogan's General Store a hundred years ago. The lady behind the counter looked as if she might have seen those days personally.

Straight gray hair in a bowl-cut framed a face creased with decades of smiling. When Matty and Sebastian came through the door, Nellie Coogan revved up that smile, the warm welcome in her brown eyes magnified by thick glasses.

Matty knew the exact moment when Nellie figured out that the bundle in Sebastian's arms was a baby. The smile faltered. With a gasp and a widening of her eyes, Nellie clutched the edge of the cash register in front of her.

"Hello, Mrs. Coogan," Matty called out, mindful of Nellie's hearing loss. "I'll bet you're surprised to see us show up with a baby."

Nellie's lips moved, but when no sound came out, she simply nodded.

"Sebastian's baby-sitting for a friend who needs some space," Matty said. "I've agreed to help him. Right, Sebastian?"

"Yep." Sebastian jiggled Elizabeth, who was kicking up a fuss under the blanket that he kept wrapped around her.

"You might want to unwrap her a little," Matty said out of the corner of her mouth. "Before she suffocates." Sometimes Nellie's hearing loss came in handy.

Sebastian drew in a sharp breath and whipped the blanket off the baby like a sculptor unveiling a statue.

Elizabeth blinked and stopped crying.

"We need to look at your baby furniture," Matty said.

Obviously still speechless, Nellie nodded again.

"Baby furniture?" asked a tall brunette who walked up to the counter with a rainbow of yarn in her arms. She dumped the skeins on the counter and turned toward Matty and Sebastian. "Baby? Where did you two come up with a kid?"

"This is Elizabeth, Gwen," Matty said. "Sebastian's agreed to baby-sit for someone who needed some space. I'm helping him."

Gwen looked almost as dumbfounded as Nellie.

"Since when does a baby-sitter have to invest in furniture?"

"This could be...for some time," Matty said. Obviously she couldn't keep the explanation as brief as she'd hoped.

Gwen raised her eyebrows. "Someone left her baby with you, Sebastian?"

"Yep."

"Have you ever taken care of a baby before?"

"Not exactly."

"That's why I'm helping him," Matty said. She tried not to laugh as she watched Gwen's expression. The wheels were turning a mile a minute in that fertile brain of Gwen's.

"You don't know much more about babies than Sebastian does," Gwen said.

"She came with instructions," Sebastian said.

"Did she, now?" Openly curious, Gwen approached Elizabeth. "Hello, there, sweetheart." She stuck her finger near Elizabeth's hand and the baby grabbed hold. "Pleased to meet you, too."

Sebastian craned his neck to get a view of what Gwen was up to with the baby peering over his shoulder. "Are your hands clean, Gwen?"

"Why, I think they're clean enough," Gwen said, her cheeks dimpling. "But if you think I should put on a surgical mask, I'll see if Nellie has one for sale. I don't have any contagious disease that I know of, though."

Matty had been thinking the same thing when Gwen made contact with Elizabeth, but Sebastian had beat her to the punch. Suddenly she wondered about all the germs they were exposing this baby to by bringing her to town. "We're new at this, and maybe a little overprotective," she said.

"That's better than being careless, or abandoning her altogether," Gwen said pointedly. "She's very young to be away from her mother. Was she being breast-fed?"

"Uh, she's on bottles," Matty said, very aware that she didn't have any with her. Gwen probably assumed they'd left the diaper bag in the car.

Gwen wiggled Elizabeth's hand. "Well, you are beautiful, Elizabeth. I can't imagine anybody needing space from *you*." She nudged the baby's nose with her own. "No, I can't. You're just precious."

Elizabeth gurgled and beamed a toothless smile.

"Sebastian!" Matty clutched his arm. "She smiled!"

"She did?" Sebastian tried to look over his shoulder and see the baby's face. He sounded miffed.

"She most certainly did," Gwen said in a musical little singsong. "Didn't you, Elizabeth? A *big* smile." She gently disentangled Elizabeth's fingers from around hers and stroked the baby's cheek with her knuckle. "What a cutie-pie."

"She never smiled for us," Sebastian said, sounding even more miffed.

"She will if you smile at her," Nellie said, shuffling slowly around the counter. She seemed to have recovered her poise. "Then she'll copy you. What sort of furniture will you be needing for that child, Sebastian?"

"A changing table," Sebastian said. "Maybe a crib."

"Come right this way." Nellie moved laboriously toward the back of the store.

Sebastian followed, and Matty started after him.

Gwen caught her arm. "Not so fast, sunshine."

Matty glanced back at her. Gwen was a good five inches taller than she was, and Matty had always thought of her as serenely beautiful. Matty envied Gwen her knack for applying makeup and arranging her long, mahogany-colored hair to her best advantage. She could wear elegant dresses that would make Matty feel ridiculous, but they fit perfectly with Gwen's role as a hostess at her Victorian bed-and-breakfast.

"What's up with that baby?" Gwen's dark gaze bored into Matty's. "Who does Sebastian know that would dump a kid on him? That seems beyond bizarre."

"I know it does, Gwen. I wish I could answer your questions, but I...can't." Matty hated being evasive with her friend, but she'd been the one who'd told Sebastian they shouldn't be too chatty with anyone until they knew more about the trouble Jessica seemed to be in.

"Wow. Then the mother's identity's a big secret?"

"Um, yeah, for now." Matty felt like a jerk. This wasn't as easy as it had seemed in the car. "I promise to tell you what's going on the minute I can."

Gwen looked hurt. "Matty, you know I wouldn't betray a confidence."

"Oh, God, I know you wouldn't." She glanced toward the back. "But—"

"You promised him you wouldn't say, didn't you?" Gwen sounded more understanding.

"Yes."

"But Matty, if you're mysterious about this baby,

people will start wondering if maybe it's Sebastian's."

Matty avoided Gwen's gaze. "Well, I guess we can't help that."

Gwen studied her for a moment. "O-*kay*. Guess we'd better drop the subject, then." She tipped her head toward the counter. "I'm going to weave myself that hooded cape we talked about."

"You are?" Matty grabbed the new topic gratefully. "I wondered when I saw all those colors you were buying. It'll be gorgeous on you, Gwen."

"I called this morning to see if you wanted to come over for coffee and help me put it on the loom, but you weren't there. I guess you were helping with the baby."

Matty hesitated. Gwen would find out sooner or later, and she needed to give her friend some information. Gwen was the only person in the world who knew how Matty felt about Sebastian. "I'm...uh... staying at Sebastian's for the time being."

"You *are?*" Gwen clapped both hands to her mouth and her eyes danced.

"But I've decided it's hopeless, Gwen."

"Because of the baby? Or should I say, the baby's mother?"

"No, that's not the problem. He came out and admitted that he's never thought of me that way."

Gwen touched her arm. "Oh, sweetie. I'm sorry."

"Until last night, that is."

"Oh, ho! Better late than never."

"Not if I'm getting Charlotte Crabtree's leftovers." Matty could feel the anger boil in her. "I think he got all excited being with Charlotte, except they didn't get to do anything, so now he's hot to trot and I'm the next race on the docket."

"Maybe."

"It's perfectly obvious, Gwen. He's starting to feel like having sex again now that he's over the divorce. Charlotte didn't work out, and now he's saddled with this baby. I've agreed to help him, so I'm handy."

Gwen considered that for several seconds. "We need to talk."

From the back of the store came a baby's wail.

"Matty!" Sebastian called as Elizabeth's crying tuned up to full volume.

"I'd better go," Matty said. "I'll send Nellie up here so you can pay for your yarn."

"Call me when you get a chance." Gwen gave her friend a compassionate glance. "And don't make too many assumptions just yet. You're pretty close to the forest."

Matty smiled rather than giving an answer. With a wave of her hand she headed to the back of the store where Elizabeth was holding court. Gwen was probably providing false hope because she didn't want to see Matty depressed. But Matty would take a little depression now rather than a permanently broken heart later.

SEBASTIAN WAS a wreck by the time he pointed the Bronco for home. They hadn't been able to get Elizabeth to stop crying, and when they admitted to Nellie they didn't have a bottle to give her, the shopkeeper suggested they buy the baby a pacifier. After a discussion about the pros and cons, he and Matty had decided in favor of the pacifier, but they weren't willing to put one straight from the store package into Elizabeth's mouth. Fortunately Nellie had offered to take it to her little apartment over the store and boil it for a few minutes.

The pacifier helped, but every once in a while, Elizabeth would spit it out and somebody had to catch it. Twice they'd missed, and Nellie had to boil the thing all over again. On the last go-round Nellie came up with a ribbon and a pin so they could pin the thing to the baby's fleece jumpsuit.

Somehow in that hullabaloo, they'd picked out a changing table, a crib, a mobile to keep Elizabeth entertained, a plastic bathtub, and at Matty's insistence, a rubber ducky and a small sock monkey. The changing-table box was behind the back seat, the crib box strapped to the roof of the Bronco, and the mobile, bathtub and toys sat in the front passenger seat.

Matty sat in the back with Elizabeth, using the monkey as a puppet while she tried to keep Elizabeth entertained during the ride home. The little girl needed changing and a meal. Both of them remembered the diaper bag they'd found among Elizabeth's belongings, and they vowed they'd never go out without it again.

"I had a monkey like this," Matty said.

"Me, too, but that doesn't mean we should have bought her one. Basic necessities are one thing, but you start buying toys, you're thinking long-term." Sebastian was ready for this exercise to be over. If he knew for a fact the kid was his, he'd adjust. Not knowing, he couldn't decide whether to get attached to Elizabeth or not.

And besides, he was no good at this baby thing. He didn't even know enough to take a spare bottle along. Matty was doing a fair job of keeping Elizabeth from crying, but he hated thinking that the little girl was hungry and sitting in a wet diaper because he hadn't come prepared.

He couldn't blame that on Matty. Jessica had left the baby with him, not Matty. Seeing that she was fed and changed and cared for was his responsibility, and he was blowing it. Jessica had placed her confidence in him because she was in some terrible trouble, and he was letting her down.

But he forced himself to drive carefully all the way home. Rain began to hit the windshield in hard little drops, and he had to slow down even more. He figured by that afternoon, the rain would become snow. If that baby caught a cold because they'd taken her out in this weather, he'd never forgive himself.

"How'd you make out with Gwen?" he asked.

"Okay. She's dying of curiosity, but I told her I couldn't give her any details yet, but I would the minute I could."

"Right." Sebastian looked forward to that day himself.

"She thinks the baby's probably yours. But Gwen's not the type to gossip."

Sebastian felt a headache coming on. "No, but that doesn't matter. Nellie is all the communication device the town needs. And the way we left town loaded with baby stuff, we might as well have taken out an ad in the *Huerfano Register*. We were noticed when we drove by the barber shop, and Jake was opening up the Buckskin right when we passed. He got a good look, so anybody who comes in for a drink tonight will hear about this."

He tried to tell himself that he didn't care what

people thought, but deep in his heart, he did care. He'd built a reputation as a straight shooter, a man of character. Although he was willing to shoulder his share of the blame for the divorce, he knew most people in the valley laid the responsibility at Barbara's feet. He'd secretly taken comfort from that whenever he'd been depressed at the failure of his marriage.

But straight-shooting men of character didn't have their illegitimate kids land on their doorstep. Besides, he was a private man, and being the subject of gossip had been one of the more unpleasant parts of getting a divorce. He thought Barbara and Butch had kept their affair quiet, but he wasn't sure, and people might have talked about that behind his back, too.

At any rate, people would have a field day with this baby appearing out of the blue. And there wasn't a damn thing he could do about it. Nothing bugged him more than a difficult situation that he couldn't do anything about. Tonight he'd call Jim about wiring the phone, in case Jessica called again.

The trip from town to home seemed to take forever, but at last he turned into the circular drive. Hard to believe that less than twenty-four hours ago he'd been cleaning house and organizing dinner. Which reminded him that Elizabeth wasn't the only one getting hungry. He and Matty had to think of their own lunch. God, he didn't know how parents of little babies got everything done.

He pulled up beside the front door and hopped out of the Bronco so he could help Matty get Elizabeth out of the infant seat. The rain had already turned to snow, but it wasn't heavy yet.

Matty handed Elizabeth to him before climbing

out herself. When he handed Elizabeth back, Matty didn't protest, as if she understood now was not the time to argue about who would do what.

"I'll change her if you'll get the bottle ready," Matty said briskly.

"Okay, but I need to unload this stuff before it starts snowing harder. I'll do it fast. Here's the key."

"Hurry." She started toward the steps.

"Right. And Matty?"

She turned, shielding Elizabeth from the blowing snow. "Yes?"

"You're a gem to do all this for me."

She smiled. "As a matter of fact, I am."

That smile worked on him while he wrestled the boxes inside. The shopping trip had distracted him for a while, but now the ache for Matty was back, and stronger than ever, as if it'd been gaining momentum while he wasn't paying attention.

On his last trip from the Bronco to the house he grabbed up the sock monkey. The minute his hand closed around the remembered texture of the monkey's body, nostalgia hit him. Damn, but he'd loved that little sock monkey he'd had as a kid. He'd called it Bruce, for no earthly reason that he could think of now. Bruce had seemed like a good name at the time. Suddenly he was glad Matty had insisted on buying it. Elizabeth should have a sock monkey.

She should also have a mother and father, he thought, shaking his head. Because he knew from bitter experience that even a sock monkey didn't take the place of that.

10

MATTY SAT IN THE ROCKER feeding Elizabeth her bottle and watching Sebastian build a fire in the fireplace. Sadie and Fleafarm dozed in cozy companionship under the dining room table as snow swirled outside, silently covering the landscape. Snow this time of year wasn't as much fun for Matty as it had been earlier in the winter, but she knew the ski resorts would be happy to get fresh powder to help them finish out the season.

She wondered if Jessica was off skiing somewhere, enjoying herself while Sebastian took care of Elizabeth. Matty didn't really believe that about Jessica. She'd heard the agony in the other woman's voice when she'd called. Still, if Jessica could turn out to be a flake who didn't want her baby, then Sebastian was free. He wouldn't try to convince a worthless mother to stay with her child.

No, he'd look for someone else to help him create the family unit he seemed to prize so much. Matty would be the logical choice. He'd already told her he prized stability over passion. As much as she'd held out for passion in marriage, Matty wasn't sure she wouldn't take his offer if it came. At least one of them would be in love.

Sebastian looked mighty good as he crouched in front of the fireplace and coaxed a flame from the logs he'd split himself last fall. His economical movements contained an easy grace that made Matty ache with longing.

Sure, she was sexually frustrated after all this time of not being with a man. But she could have rounded up someone, anyone, to satisfy that itch. Besides her date with Cyrus, she'd had veiled invitations from at least three other decent-looking cowboys since Butch died. She'd been considering whether to take one of them up on the invitation, and then Barbara had left. Since then Matty had been waiting for Sebastian.

He set the fireplace screen back in place, stood and dusted off his hands on his jeans. Then he turned to her. "Think I have time to put the crib together before her nap?"

She lowered her hungry gaze, afraid he'd notice. "I doubt it. She's already looking pretty tired. We can use the drawer one more time."

"You were right about getting the crib, though. Once we set it up we won't have to worry about the dogs so much."

She glanced toward the dining room where the dogs snoozed. "I don't worry about them, anyway. They've been perfect with her. But they might lick her and wake her up if she's on the floor. We should probably close your bedroom door while she's taking a nap."

Sebastian rubbed the back of his neck. "I don't know. I'm not crazy about having her in there all by herself with the door closed. If I thought she'd be here awhile, I'd get one of those baby monitors Nellie was talking about. I sure was amazed that she carried all that stuff. I thought we'd be lucky to get a crib, and she had nearly everything."

"You never paid attention to that part of the store. Neither did I. It's obvious Nellie loves babies. If she carries the supplies, then folks will come in with their babies."

"Makes sense. You hungry?"

"I could eat."

"Why don't I make—" He paused and continued more hesitantly. "Uh, which would you rather do, make lunch or put her down for her nap?"

"I'll make lunch," Matty said with a smile. His question was reluctant, but he was beginning to take responsibility for Elizabeth's care.

Matty eased the nipple from Elizabeth's rosebud mouth and set the bottle on the lamp table next to her. Cradling the baby more firmly, she stood. "She needs to be burped before you put her in there, though."

"I wasn't very good at that last time."

"That's why you should keep practicing. You'd better get a dishtowel for your shoulder, though. She might spit up."

He recoiled. "She might do *what?*"

"Spit up. I made the mistake of burping one of my nephews without any protection and I had to change clothes."

Sebastian looked horrified. "Are you saying she might *barf* on me? Is she sick? Should we call a doctor?"

"Not barf. Spit up," Matty said again, grinning. "It's not a condition, just something babies sometimes do when they burp. A little of the milk coming back up. It's not that gross, but you wouldn't want it on your shirt for the rest of the day."

"I'll get the dishtowel. Man, for a minute there, I

thought we'd have to head back out into the snow. You'll give me a heart attack yet, Matty Lang." Sebastian hurried into the kitchen.

She'd like to have a slightly different affect on his heart. But one thing was for sure. She couldn't leave him alone with the baby until he was more relaxed about taking care of her. From the looks of things, that wouldn't be for a while.

"Okay. I'm ready." Sebastian came back with a dishtowel draped across each shoulder.

Matty studied him. "Let's see. One baby. Two towels. Either somebody just left another baby on the front porch, or you think this kid can spit around corners."

"Very funny. I might want to switch shoulders."

"Then you switch *the towel*."

"Yeah, and while I'm doing that, I could lose my grip and drop her. How would you like to see that happen, Miss Baby Expert?"

"I think there's about as much chance of you dropping this baby as there is of Nellie Coogan giving birth. To triplets."

"I dropped Barbara's expensive crystal goblet."

"You didn't care about Barbara's expensive crystal goblet."

Sebastian grinned. "That's a fact. I like sturdy stuff. Those damn things would shatter if you looked at them wrong."

"Well, this little girl is sturdier than you give her credit for. Which shoulder do you want her on?"

"Now see there, that's the beauty of my plan. It doesn't matter."

Smiling, Matty transferred Elizabeth carefully to Sebastian, which involved no small amount of body contact. Touching him made her nerves hum with awareness.

"Hey, little girl," Sebastian said as he hoisted her to his shoulder. "Sorry we were late with your lunch. I'm just a dumb cowhand, but I promise to do better in the future."

Matty heard the deep regret in his voice and realized he felt guilty about not packing along a bottle on the trip to town. "Sebastian, we're going to make mistakes. Don't beat yourself up about it. A late bottle isn't a major problem."

"How do you know?" He started patting Elizabeth's back.

"Common sense. I think we're going to have to rely on that sometimes, considering that we don't have a lot of practical experience."

"Maybe so." He kept patting. "But once we get the furniture together, I'm reading that baby book cover to cover. I want to do this right."

And that was another reason why she was crazy about him, Matty decided as she stood there watching him pat Elizabeth's back. He might not have asked to suddenly have a baby plopped in his lap, but now that he'd been given the assignment, he'd do the best damn job possible. Sebastian was solid gold.

He wasn't bad to look at, either. A lock of his rich brown hair fell over his forehead as he adjusted his hold on Elizabeth. Matty wanted to reach over and brush it back for him. She wanted to wrap her arms around man and baby and give them both a kiss. She wanted to stay in this house with them, as snow pelted down outside and a fire crackled on the hearth, and give them all the love in her heart.

But she'd have to settle for making lunch.

"She smiled at me." Sebastian came into the kitchen as Matty was flipping over the toasted cheese sandwiches.

She glanced at him. "Really? Just now?"

"After I put her in the drawer. I guess I must've smiled at her. I wasn't really thinking about it, and then she smiled back, big as life."

"Cool." Matty felt disappointed that she'd missed the moment, but there would be other chances. One thing she didn't miss was that Sebastian looked like a proud papa standing there, telling her about Elizabeth's smile.

"What can I do?" he asked.

"Set the table, I guess. Get out some chips if you want them." She turned off the heat under the sandwiches and reached into the cupboard for a couple of plates.

He opened a bag of tortilla chips and set it on the table. "The monkey was a good idea," he said. "In fact everything you wanted to get was a good idea."

She was having trouble keeping the fondness out of her expression, so she chose not to look at him as she shoveled the sandwiches onto the plates. "You and Elizabeth were in there playing with that monkey, weren't you?"

"Oh, we might have been."

At the spontaneous note of joy in his voice, she glanced up and her heart clutched at the sparkle in his gray eyes. He was falling in love with that baby. She tried for a stern tone and failed miserably. "It's a wonder she went to sleep," she said, but there was no bite to the accusation.

"I realized that could be a problem, so I toned it

down. Then I stayed with her until her eyes closed, to make sure she'd be all right. I left the door open a crack, so we'll hear her if she wakes up."

Matty would have given anything to see Sebastian crouched beside the drawer watching Elizabeth until her eyes drifted shut. Precious moments were slipping by, moments she had no right to be a part of. She was only the helpful neighbor. Good old Matty, who would soon just be a casual visitor in this house once her services were no longer needed.

She hated self-pity, so when tears unexpectedly filled her eyes, she turned away from him, furious with herself.

"Matty, what's wrong?" He was by her side instantly.

"Nothing." Her hoarseness betrayed her. Dammit. She was about to ruin what little pleasure she could wring out of this bittersweet experience by letting him know how deeply it affected her.

"Hey." He took her by the shoulders.

She tried to twist away from him, not wanting her raw emotions chafed even more by his touch.

But he continued to hold her, gently yet insistently. "I've known you for ten years," he said softly. "I've never known you to get teary-eyed over nothing." He took her chin in one hand and turned her face up to his. "What is it, Matty?"

Gazing up at him, her vision blurred with tears, she couldn't speak.

He gazed at her silently for a heartbeat. Then muttering an oath, he lowered his head.

"No," she whispered.

"Shh."

At the touch of his lips on hers, tears spilled from

her eyes and ran down her cheeks. He gathered her close, wrapping those strong arms around her the way she'd dreamed it a thousand times. His mouth moved lazily over hers, offering comfort, warmth, caring. His arms created a safe haven from the world.

She couldn't seem to stop the tears. She didn't want comfort from Sebastian, and safety was the last thing she wanted to find in his arms. Resisting the urge to open her mouth, to invite him inside, to press her body against his in complete abandon, left her trembling.

But he was setting the pace, and his embrace was more friendly than passionate, the touch of his body almost incidental. Not that she could ever think of body contact with Sebastian in that way. Still she made herself rest her hands lightly on his chest instead of clutching his shirtfront in her fists. And she swallowed the moan that rose in her throat.

But the velvet pressure of his lips created the most exquisite torture she'd ever experienced. It was a sip of fine champagne, knowing she'd never have a full glass, a teaspoon of mocha-almond fudge ice cream, knowing she'd never have a full scoop. Yet she indulged. God help her, she focused on that sweet, not-nearly-passionate-enough kiss and memorized every second of contact.

At last he left her mouth and gently kissed her damp cheeks. He rubbed her back, not unlike the way he'd rubbed Elizabeth's back. Matty squeezed her eyes shut in frustration. She wanted his hands tearing at her clothes, cupping her bottom, kneading her breasts, slipping between her legs.

But he wouldn't do that. He was a man with incredible discipline. If he didn't think it was right to cross the line with her, then he wouldn't do it.

Gradually her tears stopped. Instead of tears she battled the ache in her breasts, the quiver in her belly and the throbbing pulse between her thighs. She braced herself for the moment that she felt certain was coming, when he would release her, step back and ask if she felt better. She wondered how she'd be able to lie convincingly while she was shaking with need.

She gulped air and tried to get her runaway heartbeat under control, but all she could think of was his mouth gliding over her face, lingering on her eyelids, feathering her wet cheeks. She wanted that mouth back on hers. And she wanted heat.

His kisses slowed, then stopped. Disappointment sliced through her. It was over.

His warm breath brushed her lips as he hesitated, probably trying to decide what to say or do that would ease them back into reality. She kept her eyes closed, knowing that one look into her eyes and he'd know everything there was to know about Matty Lang. She should slide quietly out of his arms now, but she didn't have the strength. Once he released her, she'd have a big enough challenge staying upright.

Then he groaned.

Her eyes flew open to meet his gaze. She gasped. The usually calm gray depths had been transformed. Now his eyes reflected thunderclouds before a summer storm, clouds filled with wind and lightning. Clouds heavy with rain.

"Dammit, Matty," he whispered. He backed her against the counter.

Her eyes widened. The press of his body was no longer friendly. He was completely aroused. Before she'd quite processed that information, his lips came down on hers with such force that she felt the scrape of his teeth.

She was lost. If he'd started this way she might have summoned the strength to fend him off. She might have been able to remember all the reasons why this was a bad idea. But her mind was no longer in charge. His platonic kisses had teased her beyond endurance, creating a powder keg of desire.

And he'd just lit the fuse.

With a whimper she grabbed a handful of shirt-front and opened her mouth. She'd wanted heat, and he was wildfire, scorching everything in his path. She was a willing victim of the flames. Cupping both hands behind his head, she gave and he took, possessing her mouth with a thoroughness that left her gasping.

Gone was the gentle touch that had fooled her into thinking he was in perfect control. He grasped her bottom firmly in both hands and brought her tight against his erection. When she opened her thighs and fit herself to that revealing bulge, he growled with satisfaction and nudged her back against the counter, wedging himself more firmly in the valley she created for him.

They were going to make love. She knew it the moment he pushed against her with such purpose and her body responded with that hollow, desperate need to be filled—a need so great that resisting it would be impossible. She'd kidded herself that she had a decision to make. Her body had already decided.

He didn't bother with the buttons of her shirt. Instead he pulled it from the waistband of her jeans and slipped his hands up to the back-catch of her bra. He unhooked it efficiently and slid his hands around under the material until he cradled both breasts. His touch was firm, sure, eager.

Matty thought she might pass out from the pleasure of having those work-roughened hands, hands she'd fantasized about for years, caressing her at last. Sebastian's hands. She arched into the pressure from his fingers, and a low sound of delight hummed in her throat. Oh, yes, they would make love. Wonderful, magical love.

As his thumbs grazed her nipples, bringing them to aching peaks, he lifted his mouth a fraction from hers. His breathing was ragged, his tone urgent as he kneaded her breasts. "I have to see. Undo those buttons."

Thrilled by his terse command, she fumbled with the buttons while he released her long enough to shove dishes aside. Their lunch clattered into the sink. She was only halfway done when he grasped her by her waist and lifted her to the counter.

He fumbled with the next button, couldn't get it, and in frustration pulled the shirt apart. Buttons popped, hitting sink, counter and floor as he pushed the shirt off her shoulders and down her arms. Her bra followed.

She had little time to worry whether he'd be pleased with her, but brief memories of being less than another man wanted, once upon a time, gave her a moment of anxiety. Still, there was no turning back now.

With a sigh he cupped her breasts reverently and...just...looked.

The expression on his face told her all she needed to know. This man, at least, was pleased. Well pleased. She took a trembling breath and arched her back. "Kiss me there, Sebastian." she whispered.

He settled in, and oh, how he kissed her. The brush of his lips, the slide of his tongue, the rasp of his teeth drove her slowly and surely crazy. She leaned her head against the cabinet door and tunneled her fingers through his hair while he worshiped at the altar of her breasts.

She'd been blessed with extreme sensitivity, and with Sebastian's mouth at her breast she quickly became drenched and ready. Ready to beg.

He kissed his way from her breasts up the column of her throat and found her mouth again. When he plunged his tongue inside she groaned. As if he understood, he wrapped her legs around his hips and lifted her from the counter.

"Hang on," he murmured, and carried her out of the kitchen, through the living room and down the hall.

"The baby," she whispered when he edged open his bedroom door with his foot.

His voice was a low rumble in her ear. "We'll be quiet."

She didn't think so. But she had no will of her own as he followed her down to the bed, kissing her and tugging off her jeans. She'd waited ten years to feel Sebastian deep inside her. She might never have the chance again, and she'd hold nothing back. Some things were worth the risk of waking a sleeping baby.

11

SEBASTIAN HAD SEEN the power of an avalanche, and the need sweeping through him had the same ability to wipe out everything in its path. His only hope for survival was joining with Matty, who was caught in the same wild force of nature.

He lost all interest in finesse as he tugged off one of her boots and one leg of her jeans. That was all he needed for what he had in mind, except for the barrier of her plain cotton underwear. He learned that white cotton drenched with the passionate moisture of a lady who wanted him was a hundred times sexier than black lace on an indifferent woman. The aroused scent of her made the blood surge through his veins.

But serviceable cotton didn't rip, and he was in the mood for ripping. He ended up pulling off one leg of her panties, too, which required that he pay even more attention to that part of her anatomy to get the panties off. And he was lured by her warmth, her female scent and her moist blond curls. Before he knew he meant to do it, he began kissing her there.

She tasted deliciously rich and he wanted more, but she'd begun to moan. A small part of his mind still remembered the baby sleeping beside the bed.

Easing up beside her, he covered her mouth with his, absorbing her small cry as he stroked between her thighs. He quivered and throbbed as he separated the dewy folds of her femininity, hot and swollen with passion, and found the pulsing nub guarding the entrance to paradise.

To his joy she arched her hips, meeting his questing fingers with an excitement that made him dizzy. And to think he'd wondered if she was passionate. She was the most responsive woman he'd ever held in his arms.

He pushed deeper with his fingers and his erection strained against the confining denim of his jeans. The need to free himself warred with the ecstasy of stroking her with deep, penetrating movements until she was panting against his mouth. When he rubbed his thumb across the sensitive nub, she dug her fingers into his back.

She had the grip of a woman used to riding and roping, and she was not gentle. He didn't want gentle. He wanted her mark on him, and his on her. As he continued to tease that flash point, she began to shake.

He released her mouth and nipped her shoulder, hard enough to make a bruise, and her breathing quickened, straining toward orgasm. He sucked on her breasts, raking her nipples with his teeth. Then he returned to her full mouth, drinking in her ragged breath.

Desperate though he was to plunge into her, he knew the force of his response might blind him to hers. He wanted to know Matty in the whirlwind of climax.

So he continued to caress that slick, swollen nub while he muffled her whimpers with long, soulful kisses. A moan low in her throat told him she was nearly there, and he was so wild for her that he wondered if her release would bring his.

He clenched his jaw, determined not to cheat himself of the satisfaction of sinking into her. As completion came for her, bowing her upward, he muted her cry with his mouth and probed deep, glorying in the ripple of her convulsions against his fingers.

Only when she slowly settled back to the mattress did he withdraw his fingers, trailing them up her moist body. He lifted his mouth from hers and she gulped air, her eyes still closed. Slowly he traced the outline of her mouth with a finger still moist from being deep inside her.

Her tongue edged her lips, following the path he traced. Finally the tip of her tongue slid along the length of his finger. Her eyelids fluttered open, and her eyes were the deep blue of a summer sky. Her gaze locked with his as she deliberately closed her mouth around his finger and began to suck.

A strangled sound worked its way from his throat as the pressure of her mouth and tongue blew his mind. While she licked and sucked his finger, she brought trembling hands to his shirt.

She managed to get all the buttons undone, and then she tackled his belt buckle, all the while playing games with his finger. It took her several tries to get the buckle open and an eternity to unfasten his jeans and pull down the zipper. He closed his eyes as he was hit with a wave of sensual anticipation so strong his skin felt scorched, then chilled, then scorched again. He broke out in a fine sweat.

And at last, after what seemed like a lifetime, she pushed the elastic of his briefs down and took him in both hands. He groaned, long and loud.

She lifted one hand and laid her fingers against his lips. He knew she meant to warn him to be quiet, but he began to nibble on the tips of her fingers, still needing to taste her, experience her, be with her in every way he could imagine. He'd never been so absorbed in a woman.

Slowly she eased to her side. "Lie back," she murmured in a voice so sultry he barely recognized it as Matty's.

As he rolled to his back, she came with him, rubbing his shirt aside with her silken breasts and creating an unbelievably arousing friction.

He touched every inch of bare skin he could reach while his heartbeat galloped out of control. He kissed her mouth, her breasts, her throat, as she worked herself into position astride his heat-packed body. He could barely breathe. "Condoms...in the bedside...table," he said.

"Sure thing," she murmured, brushing her breasts across his face as she reached for the drawer and pulled it open.

At the sweet contact, he moaned.

She paused, braced her hands on either side of his head and stroked her breasts across his cheek again. "Like that?" she said in a throaty whisper.

"I love that," he said hoarsely.

"Want more?"

"I want everything. Everything."

"Lift your head." She tucked another pillow under him. Then she rotated her upper body, drawing her tightly budded nipples over his lips, his eyes and his jaw while he closed his eyes and shuddered with each delicious pass. Finally she paused and fit one pert nipple between his parted lips, blatantly asking for what she wanted. He drew her in, sucking greedily.

While he enjoyed the texture and taste of her breasts, she eased her smooth bottom back and forth over his erection, coaxing him to ever higher levels of arousal. He'd never dreamed Matty could be like this. She overwhelmed him with her uninhibited lovemaking, and he was drowning in pleasure, moaning and panting shamelessly with desire.

She pulled back gently and feathered his mouth with hers. "Shh."

"I want to be deep inside you, Matty," he begged, uncaring that he sounded desperate. He was exactly that desperate. "Please get the—"

"Yes," she murmured. She took the condom from the drawer.

He was shaking like a leaf, and she didn't seem a whole lot steadier, but she took a deep breath and settled herself back on his thighs, as if she would handle the task. The way he was quivering, he was willing to let her.

She ripped open the package and took the condom out. Then she paused and wrapped her fingers around his erection. He gasped.

"You're so beautiful. I hate to cover you up." She lowered her head.

"Matty...no...." He clenched his whole body against the urge to climax when she slid her tongue just under the tip of his penis. Then she licked upward, catching the bead of moisture trembling there.

Lifting her head, she gazed at him as she ran her tongue over her lips. "You said you wanted everything."

He'd thought he couldn't be more aroused, but

he'd been wrong. He watched her through a red haze of desire as she lowered her head and repeated the motion. Oh. Yes.

All feeling became focused at the point where her tongue made contact. And flicked and made contact again. He jerked in reaction and wondered how much more he could take. More. She gathered glistening drops like a hummingbird sipping nectar. Again her head dipped. Oh, how he ached. His restraint was going...going...

"Now," he whispered when she raised her head once again.

Her blue eyes glowed. "Yes. Now."

He closed his eyes and battled for control as she put the condom on. Then the mattress shifted, and she rested her hands on his shoulders. He opened his eyes and looked up into hers. Bracketing her waist with both hands, he held her gaze as he guided her down. Her eyes were luminous. He knew he'd never forget the way they looked at this moment.

Easy. Slow. There. He drew in a sharp breath. So good. So very good. He couldn't imagine it could get any better than this.

Then she began to move, and he found out it definitely could get better. What she'd demonstrated on the dance floor she carried into the bedroom. Matty had rhythm.

The last scrap of restraint slipped away. He wanted it all, and he wasn't afraid to ask for it. "Ride me, lady," he whispered urgently. "Put the spurs to me, Matty."

Lips parted, eyes bright, she did exactly that, giving him the trip of his life. His climax rushed at him like a stampeding herd, relentlessly bearing down on him. There was no holding back—not his release or his cries of pleasure. Both erupted from him unbidden as he was swept away.

Stunned by the impact, he didn't realize for many long seconds that the fretting sound he was hearing came from the baby. Perhaps his baby. *His baby.*

"Oh no, Matty," he moaned. "What have I done?"

NO AFTERGLOW for this girl, Matty thought. Sebastian had ruined the mood. Her body might still hum with pleasure, but only because her body hadn't yet gotten the word that the party was over.

Matty figured Sebastian would have an attack of conscience eventually. She just didn't expect it to come on him the minute Elizabeth cried. She'd hoped that with the top-shelf brand of lovemaking they'd enjoyed, he'd think twice about his noble intentions to save himself for the mother of his baby. If Elizabeth even *was* his baby.

With a sigh of regret she rolled away from him and began struggling back into her clothes while he headed for the bathroom. Unfortunately she could only cover the bottom half of her. Her shirt, minus some buttons, and her bra were lying somewhere in the kitchen.

She shoved her foot into her boot and stood. "I'll be right back to help you with Elizabeth," she called. Then she went into her room, found the sweatshirt she'd thrown in the overnight bag that morning, and pulled it over her head. Her hair was still braided—barely—and her mouth felt chapped and swollen from all that unaccustomed kissing. She probably looked like a mess.

But how she looked didn't matter. Sebastian might

have let himself get carried away one time—after all, he was overdue for a roll in the hay—but now that Matty had allowed him to release that tension, he'd be strong enough to resist her. And from the deep regret in his single question, she was sure he believed that resisting her was the right thing to do.

She couldn't blame him for making love to her, which his virile body had demanded, or giving her up, which his conscience apparently required. Both decisions were totally Sebastian.

Oh, but the lovemaking had been glorious. Better than she'd imagined, and she'd imagined it would be spectacular. She finally knew how potent the combination of lust and respect could be. They had a word for that combination, she realized, and she'd never quite understood the concept until today.

The word was love.

By the time she returned to the bedroom he had clothes on and was reaching for Elizabeth.

"Wait." Matty tried not to think of their lovemaking as she looked at him, but everything came rushing back, and her body tingled, wanting more. Dammit.

He glanced up at her, his gaze guarded. "She's crying."

She remembered the open, needy look in his eyes moments ago, and swallowed a lump of despair. "I know, but she's not crying hard. She might go back to sleep if we give her the pacifier."

"Where is it?"

She suddenly felt very tired. "I think I put it in the kitchen. I'll go look."

The fire had burned down and the living room was chilly as she hurried through. The snow had stopped gusting and now fell in thick, fat flakes. A quick glance out the window revealed a hefty accumulation on the ground.

Both dogs lifted their heads and smacked their tails on the floor as she passed the dining room. "Hang on," she said. "I'll take you both out for a run in a while."

She hadn't realized until then how much she longed to get out of the house and away from Sebastian. He might have taken the edge off his desire with their lovemaking, but she'd only stoked her fire. The more she was closed in with him, the worse the longing would become. She'd struggled with her desire before, but after knowing what loving him was like, keeping her needs hidden would be torture.

The scene in the kitchen only reinforced that belief. The scattered dishes, the uneaten lunch, her blouse and bra on the floor and buttons lying on the counter made her want to scream in frustration. *Why* did he have to be so damned principled?

If Jessica had wanted him, she would have set out to get him, wouldn't she? Instead she'd left the baby and taken off. Even if the baby was his, Jessica didn't love him. And Matty did. He would be a fool to force a relationship with Jessica just to create the nuclear family he held such store by. Maybe she'd tell him that, and at least put up a fight.

She located the pacifier on the drainboard, gave it one more rinse for good measure, and took it back into the bedroom.

Sebastian was crouched next to the drawer gently rubbing Elizabeth's tummy, his brow furrowed with concern.

The fight went right out of Matty. Sebastian was bonding with this baby, and marrying her mother would be the only way he could see his child every day. Originally he might have wanted the arrangement for Elizabeth's sake, but now he might have another reason. Matty couldn't argue with him if he really wanted to be a full-time father.

She approached him and held out the pacifier. "Here."

He started to get up. "Maybe you'd better—"

"No. You try it." She shoved it toward him again. "Tease her mouth with it and see if she doesn't start sucking." Matty's pulse quickened at the flash of awareness in his eyes, and she wondered if he was thinking about the same thing she was. Everything between them could have double meanings now. As she'd imagined, it would be torture.

Without commenting, he turned back to Elizabeth and stroked the pacifier over her mouth. "She's not taking it."

"Keep trying."

He took a deep breath. "Okay, Elizabeth," he crooned as he rubbed the nipple over her rosebud mouth. "You need a little more sleep, sweetheart. Latch onto this and close those pretty eyes."

Gradually the baby stopped fussing and stared up at Sebastian. She waved her fists and gurgled before finally taking the pacifier.

"I don't really like that thing," Sebastian said as he gazed down at her.

"I know, but like Nellie said, if she's bottle-fed instead of breast-fed, she might not be getting enough sucking action to satisfy her."

"Then why didn't Jessica leave one?"

"She might have been breast-feeding until recently, when she got spooked and decided to leave Elizabeth here. She might not have needed a pacifier and didn't think to add one."

"Or she doesn't like them, either."

Irritation flashed through Matty. "Well, that's too bad if she doesn't, because she's not here to supervise. So I guess we'll have to make some decisions without her."

Sebastian shook his head. "I sure don't feel good about that."

"You're doing fine. And the sooner you assume total care of her, the better, so I can get back to the Leaning L."

He glanced up sharply, but he didn't have to ask what she meant. His understanding was plain from his sorrowful expression as he looked at her. "I'm sorry, Matty. More sorry than I can say."

Summoning what little pride she had left, she managed a smile. "Don't be sorry, cowboy. I had a great time."

"I don't want this to come between us."

She couldn't imagine how they'd ever resume their old relationship, but she wasn't about to say that now. "We'll have to make sure that doesn't happen, won't we?"

He nodded.

"But right now I could use some air. So while you make sure she goes back to sleep I'm going to take the dogs out for a run."

"In the snow?"

"I was born in this country, Sebastian. I can take the weather." She headed out of the bedroom and whistled for the dogs.

With growing despair Sebastian observed the saucy rhythm of her walk as she left the room. Only the baby lying in the drawer kept him from bellowing out his frustration as he thought of all he would miss if he couldn't make love to Matty again. Ever. And he wanted to make love to her again. Forever.

He still couldn't believe that the one he'd been born to hold had been living right down the road for the past ten years. His sense of loyalty had blinded him to her while he was married to Barbara, and for some reason he hadn't taken those blinders off, even after Barbara was gone. The divorce must have deadened his emotions more than he'd realized.

But his emotions weren't dead now. Matty had opened him up like a surprise package, and he ached to take her back in his arms, back in his bed. As luck would have it, the minute he found out what he wanted, who he wanted, the right to make that choice was taken from him by this little pink bundle gazing up at him with gray-blue eyes.

Damn, but that face was starting to look more familiar with every passing hour. The sweet baby scent of her filled him with a kind of satisfaction, and he'd become more used to the notion of picking her up. And now, each time he held her, he felt a tug in the general vicinity of his heart. Maybe that was what happened with a baby who was flesh of your flesh. Maybe nature had a way of creating that biological link.

He met Elizabeth's unblinking gaze. "Are you mine, little girl?" he murmured.

sight of old friends? She said I was spending too
much time alone. Then I said I...? I was spending
too much ... I ...

12

SEBASTIAN DIDN'T LIKE being the guilty party, and he
seemed to have it stenciled on his forehead lately.
First he'd been hit with a baby he might have created
in a drunken stupor, and now he had to face the responsibility for losing control with Matty.

Once Elizabeth drifted off to sleep, he cleaned up
the kitchen. But taking care of the mess he'd made
seducing Matty made him feel even more guilty.
And since guilt made him grouchy, he decided to
have a beer instead of eating lunch. The bite of the
amber liquid suited his mood. Then he decided the
least he could do was sew Matty's buttons back on
for her, and that demanded a second beer.

He wasn't good with a needle and thread under
the best of circumstances, and these were not the best
of circumstances. He pricked his fingers so many
times that he got blood on her shirt, tiny spots of red
sprinkled on the pink gingham. By the time Matty
came through the back door he was sewing and
swearing, but there was a cheerful lilt to his swearing. He was glad to be completing at least one job
successfully, and a little blood never hurt anything.

Standing on the mat by the back door, Matty
stomped the snow from her boots while holding the
collars of both very wet dogs, who wiggled with excitement from their run. "Maybe we should have a

couple of old towels," she said, concentrating on the dogs. "Easy, Sadie. That's a good girl, Fleafarm."

He sat gazing at her, too caught up in her wholesome beauty to think about towels for the dogs. His chest tightened with longing as he imagined what it would be like to have her coming in that back door every day, eager for his arms, his kisses, his loving. And all along she'd lived right down the road. What an idiot he'd been.

"It's cold out there, but gorgeous," she said. "There's something so refreshing about a fresh snowfall, right, girls? We saw a snowshoe bunny, didn't we? Almost caught it, too! Whoops!" She lost her grip on Fleafarm, who pranced into the middle of the kitchen and shook, spraying Sebastian.

He winced, but didn't complain. After all, he probably deserved whatever came his way.

Matty glanced at him. "Hey, I'm sorry. If you'll find me those towels, I'll—" She paused and stared at the blood-spotted shirt in his hands. "What in God's name are you doing?"

"Sewing buttons," he said. He wasn't drunk by any stretch of the imagination, but he'd had enough to blunt the pain of discovering that his life sucked. And he was to blame. "And I'll have you know I'm damn near finished with the frigging things," he said with a trace of pride.

"Oh, Sebastian." She released Sadie, who also walked into the middle of the kitchen and shook, although her short coat didn't fling water nearly as far as Fleafarm's had done. Then both dogs lapped water from their bowls and flopped to the kitchen floor, each of them giving off the musty aroma of wet dogs.

Silently Matty wound her way through the prone

dogs and headed to the round oak table where he sat. She pulled out a chair close to him and sat down. As she shrugged out of her coat and hitched it over the back of the chair, the scent of cold, pine, and that special scent that was Matty drifted his way. He took a deep breath and kept sewing, although it was tougher than usual to push the needle through the tiny holes when his hands trembled.

He wanted her. He wanted to toss aside the blood-stained shirt, stand and pull her into his arms. He wanted to kiss her until she molded herself against him the way she had before.

"You've pricked the hell out of your fingers," she said gently.

"Doesn't matter." He glanced at her briefly. Damn, she looked good, with her cheeks rubbed pink by the cold and her hair curling in damp wisps around her face. Her lips would be cool from the chilly air, but the inside of her mouth would be hot. He swallowed. "You hungry?"

"Not particularly."

"Want a beer?"

"Sure."

He pushed back his chair. "I'll get—"

"Never mind. I'll share yours." She picked up the bottle and tilted it to her full lips, her lashes drifting down as she took a sip. Then she put the bottle down and gazed at him, her eyes filled with a soft, vulnerable light. "Thanks."

He wanted her so much his throat ached. "You're welcome."

"I had some time to think, out there playing with the dogs."

"Matty, if you want to go home, then go. I'll figure

this out. And if I can't, I'll hire somebody. I can't forgive myself for bringing you into this and then..." He couldn't find the right words. "And then..."

"And then loving me better than I've ever been loved."

He glanced down, not wanting to hear that. "You probably overrated it because it's been awhile for you."

"It's been awhile, but my memory is excellent. With Butch, I always wondered if that was as good as it got. Then I'd blame myself for not being responsive enough, especially after I found out—" She stopped abruptly, clearing her throat.

His head came up. "Found out what?"

"Never mind." She avoided his gaze. "No point in discussing old history."

She knew about the affair. He was dead sure about it. And she'd never mentioned it to him because she was trying to protect him, just as he'd tried to protect her. His heart twisted. "Matty, I know about it."

Her gaze swung back to his, and the pain of that old hurt was still there. "When did you find out?"

His short laugh was directed at himself. "I would never have found out. My mind doesn't work that way. Barbara told me after she asked for a divorce."

"Oh, Sebastian." Her hand covered his. "How cruel for her to tell you then. No wonder you retreated into your shell."

He turned his hand over and held hers. He stared at those linked hands and knew that in a sane world, that would be the way he and Matty would go through life. "You found out long before that, didn't you?"

"About a week before Butch was killed." Matty

kept her attention on their joined hands, too, as if drawing strength from the contact. "We had a big argument about it the day he died. He shouldn't have been flying that day, considering the bad weather and his mental state. But hopping in that plane was an escape for him. He always said that while he was up there, his problems seemed to go away."

Sebastian lifted his head and rubbed his thumb over hers as he studied her. "You know, I've forgiven him for what he did to me, but I may never forgive him for what he did to you."

She met his gaze. "He was weak and insecure, like Barbara. But I can forgive him, especially now, thanks to you."

"Me? All I've done is mess up your life even more."

She shook her head. "You showed me that those lukewarm sessions with Butch weren't my fault. Give me the right man, and..." She smiled. "Fireworks."

He gulped.

"So here's what I was thinking while I was outside. You can send me home if I bother your conscience, but I'd like to stay. In your house...and...in your bed."

His pulse raced. "But—"

"For now," she added quickly. "I understand that if you're Elizabeth's father, you want to try to create a home with her and Jessica. I respect that." She smiled sadly. "I don't agree with it, but I respect it."

He was stunned by her offer. "Matty, there's no way I can expect you to continue what we started, knowing that I'm not free."

She squeezed his hand. "We don't know for sure

that you're not free. And if you're worried about our friendship, and our neighborly relationship, that's already screwed up. I'll never react the same to you, and you'll never react the same to me. Not after to-day." She looked deep into his eyes and her voice grew husky. "Not after the way we've touched each other."

Desire surged in him. She was right. He would want Matty Lang for the rest of his life. Even if Elizabeth turned out to be his, and Jessica agreed to marry him, he'd always long to hold Matty in his arms. But he couldn't string her along like this, even if she encouraged him to. He loved her too much.

Loved her. Life with Barbara had made him suspicious of that word, but now it seemed like the only one that fit. He loved Matty. And because he loved her, he had to protect her from the heartbreak that could come if she stayed. He had to insist that she leave.

"I can see the battle going on in those gray eyes of yours," Matty said. "And if I know you, nobility is winning."

"Matty, it's not fair for you to—"

"Don't decide yet." She gave his hand a squeeze and released it. "Think about it. And while you're thinking, remember this. I don't ever expect to have a better time in bed than I just had with you. I decided I'd be a fool to turn down the chance to repeat that experience."

He opened his mouth, but nothing came out.

"And if you had as much fun as I think you did, you'd be a fool to turn it down, too." She pushed back her chair and stood. "I'm going to check on

Elizabeth. Why don't you make us something to eat?" Then she left the room.

MATTY HAD never seen a more tortured man than Sebastian during the next few hours. Or a busier man. He turned lunch into a production and spent most of the meal on his feet adding garnishes to her plate. When it looked as if he might finally sit down with her, Elizabeth woke up, and he rushed out of the kitchen.

Putting together the changing table and giving Elizabeth a bath took the rest of the afternoon. Sebastian set the changing table up in the kitchen, and Matty didn't say a word about its placement, although she knew eventually the table should be in the same room with the crib.

She decided to wait until Sebastian was ready to assemble the crib before she suggested where to put it. She'd skimmed the baby book's chapter on sleeping arrangements and had decided that Elizabeth needed more privacy...which would give the adults more privacy, *and* that had obvious advantages. If Sebastian agreed with her, then she'd know what he'd decided to do.

Matty offered to feed the baby so Sebastian could work on the crib. Both Sadie and Fleafarm settled at Matty's feet once she sat down with Elizabeth. Sometime during the day, they'd decided Elizabeth was their responsibility, too, and wherever the baby went, they went. Matty had noticed the same instincts in her sister's dogs, so she wasn't surprised.

As Sebastian picked up the box containing the crib and started toward his bedroom, Matty called to him, as if something had just occurred to her.

"Maybe you should set that up in the guest room, instead," she said casually.

He stopped dead and lowered one end of the box to the floor. Then he turned to her, his gaze speculating. He obviously wasn't fooled by her casual tone. This was a loaded topic, and he knew it. "You mean your room?"

If he agreed to her proposition, it wouldn't be her room any longer. And they didn't want to worry about waking up the baby if they made love. But she wasn't ready to be quite so blunt.

She ignored his reference to *her* room. "At first I thought she needed to be in the same room with you," she said. "But I read a section in the baby book Jessica sent, and it advises parents to give the baby her own room, if possible. She sleeps better, and the adults...sleep better."

"Interesting that you'd take the time to check out that section."

"Well, you've been very busy, so I figured you wouldn't have a chance."

"Ah, Matty." He sighed, obviously torn between his desire and his conscience. "The book really said she needs privacy?"

"It really said that."

He hesitated. "Maybe I could put her in my office."

"You could, but it's farther from your room. You might have to go to her in the middle of the night."

He glanced down the hall, then over at the grandfather clock in the corner of the living room. "I guess it's too late to call Jim. He's probably headed home for dinner by now."

She didn't follow the abrupt change of subject.

"You mean to fix the phone, so you can track Jessica if she calls?"

"Yeah, for that, and an intercom for the baby. And a security system."

"A security system? You have two dogs who have attached themselves to this baby."

"Yeah, but I've been thinking."

No joke. It's a wonder smoke isn't coming out your ears. "And?"

"The dogs are fine for normal security, but if someone's after Jessica, they might find out about Elizabeth and try to get to Jessica through her baby. If they're sophisticated enough, a couple of dogs won't stop them."

A chill zipped down Matty's spine and she glanced at the soft, vulnerable baby in her arms. "I hadn't thought of that."

Elizabeth gazed up at her and patted her tiny hands against the sides of the bottle as she drank. She was completely helpless, with no choice but to trust Matty and Sebastian to keep her safe.

That responsibility settled over Matty's shoulders, and she gave up her dream of creating a private love nest with Sebastian. "Maybe you'd better put the crib in your room after all," she said. She could order priorities, too, and the baby's safety came ahead of everything else.

"Yeah, I think I will for now. At least until I can get Jim out here to do some wiring."

"Then we should probably put the changing table in there, too. And the box with her clothes and diapers in it."

"I'll do that after I set up the crib." He lifted the box and carried it down the hall.

Before long Matty heard the clunking and clacking noises of furniture being assembled. "Looks like you and Sebastian will be roomies again, Elizabeth," she told the baby. "The question remains as to whether I'll be invited in, too."

Elizabeth patted the bottle and stared up at Matty.

"You know, when you look like that, as if you're thinking deep thoughts, you remind me a lot of the guy in there building your crib. I guess you could be his, after all." Matty nestled the baby more securely in her arms and tilted the bottle to a sharper angle. "He got you a real girlie crib, Elizabeth. I tried to talk him into the basic model, pine finish, simple yet tasteful, gender-neutral. But he went for the froufrou pink-and-white one."

Elizabeth blinked and stopped sucking on the bottle.

"See? I knew you'd be horrified by that sugar-and-spice junk. You'd rather have the pine finish, right?"

Pushing the nipple out of her mouth, Elizabeth signaled she'd had enough.

Feeling almost like an old hand, Matty put down the bottle and lifted Elizabeth to her shoulder, where she'd already spread a dishtowel. Then she started patting and rubbing the little girl's back.

"I can tell you're not gonna be a froufrou kind of girl," she said. "No dolls and tea parties for you. *Boring.* Hideouts and secret codes, that's what's happening. I'll tell you a story from my naughty childhood if you promise not to blab." She turned her head to kiss the incredibly soft little cheek.

Elizabeth gurgled in response.

"Sounds like a promise to me. Well, my aunt Georgia insisted on giving me a doll, even when I told her

I didn't want one. And let me tell you, this was one ugly doll. Well, one night my folks took us to see a melodrama, and the next day my brother talked me into tying that doll to the railroad tracks about two blocks from our house.

"Somebody found her before the train went by, and my brother and I got in *big* trouble. But I never got another doll, either, which was fine with me."

The baby erupted in a loud burp.

"Well done," Matty said. "Don't you ever worry about being dainty, Elizabeth. Dainty is highly overrated in my opinion. I just hope that fancy-dancy crib doesn't mess with your head. You have to forgive Sebastian. He only had a brother and he has some stereotypical ideas about girls. I'll work on him." *If I get the chance.*

She didn't know which way Sebastian would go, whether he'd decide to seize the day—and night—or send her home to soothe his over-developed conscience. But at least she hadn't run out like some fraidy cat, which had been her first impulse. Getting outside into the crisp Colorado air had cleared up her fuzzy thinking and let her see that going home lacked courage.

Maybe Sebastian would break her heart, but maybe he wouldn't. And in the meantime, the two of them could make memories that would last a lifetime. Sure, it was risky, but Matty had yet to find a sure thing in this world. She'd pay her money and take her chances. If Sebastian would cooperate.

ALL THROUGH the afternoon Sebastian kept thinking they'd get to a place where he'd be able to say that yes, he could handle it from here. He could take care

of Elizabeth, and Matty could go home. He believed
that was the best course of action, but he was afraid
to have her walk out until he was sure he could make
it through the night.

And now the day was gone, and while he thought
he might be able to go solo now, he wasn't keen on
sending Matty out into a snowstorm after dark.
While he put Elizabeth to bed with both dogs sta-
tioned under the crib, Matty made them a light sup-
per and set it on the coffee table in front of the fire.
Very cozy.

Desire stirred in him just looking at the intimate
arrangement. He pictured how Matty would look
with firelight on her naked body, and his blood ran
hot. But he didn't think it was in Matty's best interests to cozy up to him at this point in his life, no matter what she'd said earlier in the day.

They ate in silence while he struggled with how to
broach the subject. Finally he set his empty plate on
the coffee table in front of the sofa and rested his
arms on his knees, staring into the flames. "The snow
never did let up."

"No, never did." She set her plate beside his and
curled up against the plump cushions, her sock-cov-
ered feet tucked under her, her boots on the floor
next to the sofa. She looked so soft and welcoming,
so ready.

He remembered how ready she could be. His
groin tightened. He forced his mind away from the
erotic images that had simmered in his subconscious
all day, and took a deep breath. "Matty, I don't think
it would work, what you suggested right before
lunch."

"Because you don't really want me?"

He shot her a glance. "You know better than that."

"Not really."

"I'm thinking of you, Matty. It's a dead end. The more I look at Elizabeth, the more I'm convinced she's mine. I think it'd be best if we cut it off clean between us now."

Matty sighed. "Well, if you're not interested, then you're not interested. Simple as that." She reached for her boots and started pulling them on. "I think you're in decent shape for taking care of Elizabeth, so I'll be toddling on home."

"That's just it. I don't want you driving home in this. The road will be a nightmare."

She pulled on her second boot. "I can make it home. My truck has four-wheel drive, and I've driven in worse weather than—"

"I don't care. I don't want you to do it."

She glanced over at him. "Too bad, cowboy. I'm not staying in that guest room another night. Sadie and I are going home. I'll just go get her." She stood and started out of the living room.

"Dammit, Matty, don't be bullheaded." He followed her down the hall. "We can make it through one more night, and I can follow you home tomorrow, to make sure you don't end up in a ditch."

She kept walking. "Forget that. I'll call you when I get home. If you don't hear from me for an hour, you can call for a tow truck and ask them to look for me. It's not a long stretch. I'm sure they'd find me." She pushed open the bedroom door that he'd partially closed and walked through the darkened room to the crib, where Sadie and Fleafarm were on guard underneath it.

Sebastian pictured Matty's truck in a snowbank

with her inside, and his chest tightened with the beginnings of panic. "No," he whispered fiercely, grabbing her arm. "You're smarter than that, Matty. These storms—"

She turned to him, her eyes glittering from the light coming through the door. Her voice was a low hiss. "If you think for one minute that I'm going to stay across the hall like a good girl because you don't have the *cojones* to make love to me, then you're not so smart either."

"You think I don't want to make love to you?" he said sharply.

"That's what I think. You got some relief from your long dry spell today, and that was all you needed from me."

With a low growl of frustration he pulled her into his arms. "You don't know anything, Matty Lang."

She lifted her chin in challenge. "Oh, yeah? Then prove it."

13

Sebastian shoved her to the bed so hard she bounced, but her booted feet stayed on the floor. Before she could react, he was on her, pressing her to the bed with his upper body while he wrenched open the fastening on her jeans.

Heat and excitement surged through her. She'd reined in her desire all day, but with his first frenzied touch it broke free. He brought her to a fever pitch faster than she'd ever dreamed possible.

He put his mouth close to hers, but not to kiss her. "You are the most bullheaded female I've ever met," he said, breathing hard. "So I'm going to prove how much I want you, Matty. Right here. Right now. And if you wake up that baby while I'm doing it, you're going to walk the floor with her afterward, not me."

Her heart was pounding and her ears were ringing. She was so aroused that her voice shook. "Sebastian, don't you think we should—"

"Shut up. I'm running this show." Using both hands, he pulled her jeans and panties down in one efficient sweep. Then he slid to his knees on the floor at the end of the bed, grasped her hips, and pulled her toward him. Without any further preliminaries he lowered his head and began to plunder her most secret place.

Ravished. It was the only way she could think

about what was happening to her. And then she couldn't think at all as he turned her into a flame burning hot and fast. She pushed her fist against her mouth.

He was relentless, driving her higher and higher with a thoroughness that made her gasp and see stars. His fingers dug into her bottom, holding her steady while she quaked in his grip and arched shamelessly toward the ecstasy he promised. No man had ever shown her passion like this. Her head thrashed from side to side and her skin flushed as if she lay under the noonday sun.

Teasing wasn't part of the deal. He pushed her straight toward the edge of the cliff, and when she fell, she bit down hard on her knuckle to keep from yelling.

As she lay limp and quivering, she felt the stir of air when he stood, heard the scrape of wood on wood as he opened the bedside table drawer, the chink of his belt buckle as his jeans hit the floor. Then he was back, pulling off her boots, jeans and panties with more tenderness than urgency.

Lifting her like a rag doll, he eased her up higher on the bed. As he moved between her thighs, a shadowy lover, he leaned down and kissed her.

She'd thought her passion had been spent on that rocket ride he'd just provided, but the taste of love was on his mouth, and heat licked through her again, lighting fires all along the way. Her body began to throb to a new rhythm as his tongue probed deep. His erection brushed the outer folds of her pulsing femininity.

He lifted his mouth a fraction from hers. "I want to

make love to you, Matty, in every way you could imagine, but especially like this." He pushed home.

She moaned softly at the pleasure of that perfect connection.

"I wouldn't have slept at all, knowing you were in that guest room." His warm breath caressed her mouth. "You drive me crazy." He moved slowly, easing back and rocking forward, sending shock waves along her system with every lazy undulation.

"So...you...want me to stay?" she said breathlessly.

"Tonight." He nibbled at her lower lip as he kept up the sensuous rhythm. "But I want you to leave tomorrow."

"No." Pain knifed through her at the thought. He was still hell-bent on protecting her.

"Yes."

"No." She couldn't give this up. This magic. This unbelievable joy. "If...it comes to nothing...I can take it."

His voice roughened. "You know, I think you could. You're tough." He shifted the angle slightly and increased the pressure. His breathing grew ragged. "But...I...can't." Then his mouth came down hard on hers as he stepped up the pace, bringing her with him as he catapulted them both over the edge.

A CLEAN BREAK with Matty was impossible, Sebastian realized as he struggled through the following three weeks. They'd been neighbors for ten years and were used to relying on each other. Matty called him when she was concerned about one of her geldings. He called to see if he could borrow her clothes-dryer when his went on the fritz and Elizabeth had run out of clothes.

And although he had most of the basics of baby care down, he still needed to consult with someone about Elizabeth, and Matty was the person he trusted. Mostly they talked on the phone, but a few times he needed her to come over, and once he desperately required her help when he went shopping for diapers and formula.

During those times they concentrated on the baby as best they could, but he ached with longing and he figured Matty did, too. Even without Elizabeth interrupting his sleep at odd hours, he wouldn't have slept well. His nights were filled with dreams of Matty. Most were X-rated, which was frustrating enough, but the most heartbreaking ones featured Matty as the mother of her own child. Of their child. He awoke from those dreams with a pain so real that he groaned aloud.

No doubt about it, he'd experienced the purest happiness he'd ever known with a woman during the brief time Matty had stayed at the Rocking D. And he had little hope that he'd ever recapture that happiness. Elizabeth was his daughter. He was sure of it.

To add to his restless feeling, a warm breeze blew across the face of the Rockies, hinting at a spring that was still a couple of weeks away, but was definitely coming. He looked for buds on the aspens in the front yard and imagined he could see the bark swelling, but no green leaves appeared. At least one more snowstorm would probably hit before spring really took hold, but the air was fresh with promise when he stepped out on the porch every morning, and sexual urges rose in him like sap.

In a week he'd be thirty-five-years old. Hell, he'd expected to be dealing with teenagers by this point in his life. Instead he spent his time taking care of one little baby who might or might not be his. He wanted more children. With Matty.

He'd never planned to have Elizabeth this long without knowing more about her parentage and Jessica's problem. Jessica had called once more, but after he'd told her the baby was fine, she'd hung up. Sure, he'd traced the call, but a pay phone in Phoenix wasn't much to go on. It looked more and more as if he'd have to hire a private investigator.

Out of necessity, he'd worked out a routine for taking care of Elizabeth, and a baby carrier strapped to his back allowed him to pack her along while he handled his chores. He wasn't sure what he'd do if she was still here when the cattle arrived and he needed to start riding again. He'd cross that bridge when he came to it. For now he took things day by day, hoping that Jessica would show up.

And he wanted her to show up. Of course he did. He needed to know for sure if he was Elizabeth's father. But if Jessica did come back and tell him the baby wasn't his, and that she was ready to take Elizabeth, Sebastian wasn't sure how he'd feel about that. It would mean he was free to go to Matty, but it would mean losing Elizabeth.

Three weeks ago he would have accepted that, probably with some relief that he was off the hook. But now...now was a different story. Elizabeth recognized him, and her little face lit up when she saw him coming. Smiles had become laughter, and she cooed to beat the band when he played with her. She'd started making sounds that some day would be words. Words like *daddy*.

And then, tonight when he'd put her in the crib for a minute while he checked on dinner, he'd returned to find that she'd rolled over.

"Hey, super baby!" He scooped her up, praising her to the skies while she gurgled happily in his arms. Cradling her against his chest, he hurried across the bedroom and grabbed the phone. Matty had to hear about this.

He waited impatiently for her to pick up and didn't even bother identifying himself. "Matty? She *rolled over*."

"Really?" Matty laughed with delight. "Front to back, or back to front?"

"Back to front." Sebastian was so excited he was breathing fast. "But I'll bet she could do it the other way. Matty, she's so smart. She's the smartest little baby in this valley."

"I could have told you that." Matty's warm voice poured over him. "Put her on."

"Here she is." As they'd done several times before, Sebastian held the receiver to Elizabeth's ear. As he listened to Matty congratulate Elizabeth on her milestone, the baby grinned and wiggled in his arms.

He wanted Matty there. She should be there, sharing this moment with him. Damn, but he needed her. Nothing about this arrangement felt right to him anymore, and in a flash he knew with absolute certainty that he could never marry Jessica. Which meant—oh, God, he wasn't sure what it meant, except that he needed to see Matty tonight, needed to tell her—

The doorbell rang.

A chill of premonition ran up his spine. Jessica. Maybe the moment of truth had arrived.

He brought the receiver back to his ear. "Somebody's at the door," he said. "I'll call you back."

"Okay." She sounded wary, as if she'd picked up on his tense reaction to the doorbell.

"You'll be home?"

"Sure."

"Okay. 'Bye." He hung up the phone as the doorbell pealed again. Taking a deep breath, he headed for the front door.

Elizabeth kept her head up really well now, and she looked around with interest as he walked with her. Fleafarm trotted beside him, on alert.

Sebastian had developed the habit of drawing a section of curtain aside and glancing out the front window to see who was standing on the porch before he opened the door. Normally, country living didn't require so much caution and he resented the need for it, but until he knew what dangers might threaten the baby, he would be careful.

When he drew back the curtain and peered out, he blinked in disbelief and hurried to the door. He flung it open and stared at Travis Evans, who stood on the porch holding the biggest stuffed purple giraffe Sebastian had ever seen. With yellow spots. It was nearly as tall as Travis, who was close to six feet.

Travis stared back, but his light brown eyes weren't focused on Sebastian. All his attention was riveted on Elizabeth, and there was no surprise in his expression.

Sebastian got a sick feeling in his gut.

Fleafarm, one of Travis's devoted female admirers, dashed through the door with a yip of delight.

"Hey, Fleafarm." Travis took his gaze from the baby long enough to lean down and scratch behind the dog's ears while Fleafarm wiggled happily.

"What the hell are you doing here?" Sebastian asked, hoping for a different explanation than the one he was afraid was coming.

"Oh, I was in the neighborhood." With a final pat for the dog, Travis walked through the door carrying the giraffe by the neck.

"I take it that's not a birthday present for me."

"Nope. It's for Lizzie, there."

So he knew her name. The sick feeling in Sebastian's stomach grew. "Who told you about her?"

"A little birdie." Propping the giraffe against the wall, he took off his Stetson and put it on the stuffed animal.

"Matty?" He hoped it was Matty. In fact, logically it could be Matty. Travis might have called to check on the schedule for picking up the cattle, and found out about Elizabeth that way. But that wouldn't explain why he was here, Sebastian thought, as his gut churned some more.

"No, not Matty." Travis pulled a crumpled piece of paper out of his jacket pocket. "I would've been here sooner, but this got delivered to the wrong address and I just got it three days ago. It's from Jessica."

Sebastian clutched Elizabeth tighter as he eyed the familiar-looking stationery. Until that moment, he hadn't realized how much he'd clung to the belief that this precious little bundle was his daughter. "And?" His voice was hoarse with strain.

Travis ran his fingers through his wavy brown hair. His tawny gaze lost some of it's usual cockiness. "She wrote to me and asked me to be the godfather to this baby until she can come get her, but we all know what that means. It's mine."

Relief roared through Sebastian. "The hell it does! Let me see that." He snatched the paper from Travis and quickly skimmed the message:

Dear Travis,
I'm counting on you to be a godfather to my daughter Elizabeth until I can return for her. Your playful approach to life is just what she needs right now. I've left her with Sebastian at the Rocking D. Believe me, I wouldn't do this if I weren't in desperate circumstances.
In deepest gratitude,

Jessica

Sebastian read the message again and swore softly.

"See, I figured out what must've happened," Travis said. "That night we all got trashed at the avalanche reunion party I made a pass at her, when she was tucking me into bed. The rest is hazy, but I figure Jessica and I did the nasty. I was too drunk to use birth control. Hell, I was too drunk to remember doing it, but apparently my automatic pilot works pretty good."

Sebastian gazed at him. No telling what was going on here, but at least Jessica hadn't out-and-out named Travis as the father. He handed the note back. "Hang on for a minute. I need to get something. Oh, and you might as well take off your jacket and grab a beer if you want one. We have some talking to do."

"Oh." Travis scratched the back of his head. "Then I need to use your phone to call Deb and cancel."

"You made a *date* for tonight? When you were coming to town to claim this baby as yours?"

Travis shrugged. "I brought her a giraffe, didn't I? It's not like I'd know what the hell to do with her, so I didn't figure I'd be the designated baby-sitter. I'm sort of surprised to see you doing the honors, to be honest. I thought you'd get somebody like Matty to take over."

Which he had, at first. But that gave him all the more reason to resent Travis's casual remark. "She has a lot better things to do than worry about this baby, you know," he said. "For your information, Matty is a very talented woman, not just some handy person you can rope in as a nursemaid when the occasion arises."

"Whoa!" Travis gave him a puzzled glance. "I didn't say she wasn't talented. I know Matty's fantastic. I work for her every summer, remember? Matter of fact, I always wondered why you never considered...well, never mind. That's none of my business."

"Damned right it isn't," Sebastian muttered as he headed back to his bedroom, Elizabeth bouncing on his shoulder.

"Baby-sitting makes you grouchy, Sebastian." Travis followed him. "Hey, Lizzie! You are a cute little thing, aren't you? Figures you would be. You've got the Evans' hair."

"Hell if she does," Sebastian mumbled. He

couldn't figure out why Jessica had dragged Travis into this, but he didn't like it one damn bit. And the two of them would need to get some things straight pronto.

To be fair, maybe Jessica hadn't wanted Sebastian to handle this all by himself. Before too long it would become a problem—when he had to start running cattle, as he did every summer. Maybe Jessica thought that Travis, being one of his best buddies and a good friend of hers, too, would be the logical one to share the burden.

Still, Sebastian didn't care for the way she'd worded Travis's note. *Your playful approach to life is just what she needs right now.* As if Travis knew how to play with this tiny baby. He'd brought her a stuffed animal ten times bigger than she was. Elizabeth did fine with a sock monkey and a rubber ducky. She didn't need a six-foot purple giraffe, that was for sure.

"Hey, Lizzie. Watch this. I can touch the tip of my tongue to my nose."

"I'm sure she's impressed," Sebastian said.

"All the girls like that," Travis said. "Oh, my God. She's smiling at me. Damn, but that's cute."

"That's gas," Sebastian said.

Elizabeth cooed.

Well, that's gratitude for you, Sebastian thought as he laid her on her back in the crib and she continued to gaze adoringly at Travis. Sebastian had worked his fingers to the bone taking care of her, and she smiled at the first guy who came along who could touch his tongue to his nose.

"You have a whole damned setup here, don't you?" Travis said to Sebastian as he glanced around.

"Baby-central. Did Jessica leave all this stuff with you?"

"Nope." Sebastian searched the clutter on the top of his dresser. Lately he'd been completely disorganized, but he thought that was where...aha. He unearthed Jessica's note and turned back to Travis.

"So you bought all this? The crib and that shelf thing, and—"

"Changing table."

"Yeah? What does it change into?"

Sebastian sighed and shook his head. If this was Jessica's idea of sending in the troops, she should have left well enough alone. He'd have to spend so much time educating Travis it wouldn't be worth the effort.

"Oh, I get it. You change her diapers on that table. That's what the cinch is for."

"Just see that you don't put your knee in her belly before you tighten it down, cowboy."

"Don't worry about that. This boy's not changing no stinkin' diaper."

Sebastian had a new point of reference these days. Not that he really wanted Travis fooling with the kid, but it was the principle of the thing. Travis should want to do his part, even if Sebastian wasn't planning to let him. He fixed Travis with a steely stare. "And why not change her diaper?"

"Not in my job description," Travis said smugly. "I'm supposed to give Lizzie my playful attitude toward life. That's fun and games, not maintenance."

"You might want to rethink that, *godfather*." He handed Travis Jessica's note.

Travis's took the paper and compared it to the one in his hand. His jaw dropped. "I'll be damned," he murmured. He glanced up. "Then she didn't talk to you when she dropped off the kid?"

"She drove up one night, left Elizabeth on the porch and rang the bell. When I went to the door, she drove off like a bat out of hell."

"Hellfire." Travis gazed at Sebastian. "What's going on here?"

"Damned if I know. Before you showed up, I figured I was Elizabeth's father."

Travis blinked. "No way, Jose. Not straight-and-narrow Daniels. You couldn't have—"

"Oh, yes, I could," Sebastian said heatedly. "The last thing I remember about that night was trying to kiss her."

"A kiss? Hell, a kiss is nothing. Everybody knows when it comes to real action, I'm the guy."

"Why are you so eager to claim her? You need a baby to support like you need another hole in the head."

Travis nodded. "True. When I first got the letter, I panicked. I have no intention of getting tied down, not to a wife, and certainly not to a baby. But after I'd read that note a few times, I figured out what Jess is trying to do."

"Then you'd better clue me in, because I don't have the foggiest idea."

"She knows I'm not looking to be tied down, so she didn't even tell me when she got pregnant. I think she should have, but she didn't. Probably never would have told me Lizzie was mine."

"Her name's *Elizabeth*, dammit."

"We'll see about that. Anyhow, Jess is in some kind of trouble, and she needs temporary help with the kid. She would have left her with me, except your place was more convenient and easier to find. Mine's not, which is why the letter got lost in the first place."

"I think you have it all wrong." Sebastian had taken pride in the fact that Jessica had left Elizabeth with him, the guy she could trust to be in charge. He didn't want to believe he'd only been more convenient than Travis. He didn't want to believe Travis was Elizabeth's father, either.

"I think I've got it about right," Travis said. "So here I am, to do my part for the kid, and for Jess. Maybe this baby was an accident, but by God, I'll shoulder my responsibilities."

Sebastian clenched his jaw. "She's not yours."

"Sure she is."

"She has my eyes."

"And my hair."

"And the Daniels' nose."

"And the Evans' sense of humor!"

As they stood there glaring at each other, Elizabeth began to fuss. They both turned to look at the crib.

"She doesn't sound very happy," Travis ventured.

"Probably because she needs her britches changed," Sebastian said, a challenge in his voice. He didn't really want Travis here, but if he insisted on staying, then maybe he should change a few diapers, after all.

Travis started backing out of the room. "Uh, well, I'd be glad to help you out, there, Sebastian, but I have to go call Deb. You know how women hate getting stood up."

Sebastian snorted in disgust. "I don't know what

you're so scared of. You've must've mucked out thousands of stalls in your day."

"Hey, there's a thought! I'll take care of your horse manure, and you take care of the baby's...uh... output. Teamwork!"

Sebastian shook his head. "I don't have any idea what Jessica had in mind when she sent you that note, but if you're planning to stick around, you're not sliding by with tongue tricks. You're gonna do the tough jobs, too."

"But I don't know the first thing about—"

"And I'm just the guy to teach you. I don't have the energy tonight, but the first diaper of the day tomorrow has your name on it, cowboy."

Travis shrugged. "If you're so all-fired set on it, I'll take a turn." Then he left the room to make his call.

He wasn't the only one who should make a call, Sebastian thought as he lifted Elizabeth gently from the crib and put her on the changing table. He'd promised to call Matty back, and besides, she deserved to know this latest development. But he hesitated to call her until he'd worked everything out in his mind. Travis showing up had knocked him off-kilter.

Matty would be quick to point out that Travis's note let Sebastian off the hook. He couldn't assume he was Elizabeth's father any more than Travis could. Although he wasn't about to admit it to Travis, there was a good chance neither of them was the father.

That was logic talking. Sebastian gazed down at Elizabeth. "What do you say, Elizabeth? What do you say, pretty girl?" Her serious stare was so cute he couldn't help smiling.

She smiled back, gave a little croak of happiness and waved her fists at him.

Sebastian's heart twisted. "I don't care about the evidence," Sebastian murmured. "You're my baby."

14

"I'M NOT SURE this is a good idea." Matty climbed
into Gwen's violet truck anyway. Sebastian hadn't
called her back after all, and she had to know who
had been at his door the night before.

"My curiosity's aroused. I want to know who was
at the door, too. And I can't help you decide what to
do unless I've seen how Sebastian acts around you."
Gwen put the truck in gear and pulled away from
Matty's house. "Delivering the baby blanket is the
perfect excuse."

"You don't need me to do that."

"No, but he knows we're friends, and we'll tell
him we're out running errands together today.
Dropping off the blanket happens to be one of
them."

"I wonder if he'll see through that story." Matty
stroked the baby blanket on her lap. Gwen had spent
the past three weeks weaving a masterpiece for Elizabeth in shades of pink, blue and lavender.

Matty wished she'd been able to concentrate long
enough to complete a project like that for the baby,
but her frustration level was too high. The few times
she'd tried to weave anything she'd made a tangled
mess of it, so instead she'd spent her time doing
heavy physical work, getting a jump on repairs in
preparation for the busy summer season.

"I hope he does see through our story," Gwen said. "But I wouldn't count on it. The man seems attached to those blinders he wears."

"It's because he still thinks he can create the perfect family group if he tries hard enough." Matty hadn't confided the particulars about Elizabeth's mother, but she had confirmed Gwen's suspicion that Sebastian thought he was the baby's father. Gwen shared Matty's frustration with Sebastian's sense of duty to a woman who'd merely dropped the baby on his doorstep, a woman he didn't even love.

"The perfect family group." Gwen shook her head. "Now *there's* a fantasy if I ever heard one. Derek taught me how unrealistic that dream is."

Matty sighed. "We haven't had the greatest luck in men, have we, Gwen?"

"Nope." Gwen turned down the lane leading to the Rocking D. "But I'll say this much for Sebastian—he's not a runaround like Butch and Derek turned out to be. At least you're not looking to repeat your mistake by falling for the same type of rascal you had before. If you'd set your cap for somebody like your head wrangler, I'd be worried about you."

Matty laughed. "Travis is harmless. He just wants to have fun."

"Oh, I wouldn't call him harmless. God gave him too many weapons to use in the war between the sexes, and he's mastered all of them. That heavy-lidded glance he gives you, the loose-hipped way he walks, the macho way he sits a saddle. No, not harmless. The guy should be forced to wear a warning sign around his neck."

Matty glanced at her friend and couldn't help smiling. "I didn't know you were attracted to him."

"To Travis?" Gwen hooted. "Travis would be the last man on earth I'd allow myself to be attracted to. I have no interest in living through Derek, Part Two."

"Oh, I get it." Matty's grin widened. "You *would* be attracted to Travis if you allowed yourself to be, but you don't allow yourself, so you're not."

Gwen glared at her. "Do I look like an idiot? Those who don't admit to their mistakes are doomed to repeat them. I've meditated extensively on this subject, and as a result of deprogramming myself, Travis and all members of his tribe completely turn me off."

"Uh, huh." Matty paused. She liked Travis as a friend and felt pushed to defend him. "For what it's worth, I've never known Travis to deceive anyone. Seems to me there's a difference between a man who frankly and openly enjoys women, and one who pretends to be monogamous and then swipes from every available cookie jar."

"Maybe, but I don't have any use for either brand. And the third kind, the ones who promise to love and cherish and actually follow through on the promise aren't all that thick on the ground, in my experience."

"Huerfano's a small town. Your selection is limited."

"I know, but I love it here, and I'm not giving up the peace and serenity I've found in Huerfano to travel the world looking for that true-blue guy who wants to settle down and raise babies."

Matty remembered the wistful look on Gwen's face when she'd played with Elizabeth in Coogan's Department store. Then Gwen had gone home and started weaving a baby blanket instead of the colorful material for the cape she'd planned to make for herself.

Tracing the intricate pattern in the blanket, Matty wondered if Gwen was as peaceful and serene as she claimed, or if her heart ached to weave blankets for her own babies. But she'd been burned by Derek. She was probably afraid to try again.

Gwen's soft oath caused Matty to glance up as they pulled up in front of Sebastian's house.

"That's what we get for speaking of the devil," Gwen said. "I guess we know who came to Sebastian's door last night."

Matty stared at Travis Evans's muscle truck parked in the circular drive. The truck looked as if it had been driven hard to get here. Dried mud covered the custom black and silver paint-job and the Utah license plate.

Not only was Travis several weeks early, he'd changed his usual pattern of arrival. Ordinarily when he returned to Colorado for the summer, he came to Matty's place first to stow his gear in the bunkhouse.

"Maybe Sebastian and Travis had something planned I didn't know about, like another ski trip," Matty said. "Sebastian's birthday is next week. Maybe he didn't notify Travis that the plans would have to change." She watched Fleafarm bound around the side of the house and come toward the truck wagging her tail.

"Possible, but I have the feeling this has something to do with that baby in there."

Matty unlatched her seat belt and opened her door. She had the same feeling Gwen did, and her chest tightened with anxiety. If there had been a new development, Sebastian should have had the courtesy to call her.

She'd held onto the belief that if Sebastian discovered Elizabeth wasn't his, or even had increased doubt about it, he'd reconsider his position in regard to Matty because he really cared about her. But if Travis had arrived because of a new development, and Sebastian hadn't called, then maybe he didn't care as much as she thought.

There was only one way to find out what Travis's presence meant. She hurried from the truck, clutching the blanket under one arm as she reached down absently to pet Fleafarm.

Belatedly she remembered the blanket was a gift from Gwen and she shouldn't carry it into the house. She turned back, handing it over with a sheepish smile. "Here. You're the one who should give him this, not me."

"Um, yeah. Right." Gwen took the blanket, but she looked as distracted as Matty felt. After greeting Fleafarm, she adjusted the clip holding her long dark hair, which was about as close to primping as she ever got.

Even in her rattled state, Matty noticed that her friend was at least as nervous as she was. Now that she thought about it, Travis and Gwen hadn't been in each other's company much. That was logical, because summer was Gwen's high season at Hawthorne House, and in the winter when she had more leisure time, Travis was in Utah. Still, Matty was beginning to wonder if Gwen had deliberately avoided being near him the way a recovering alcoholic might avoid being near a bottle of whiskey.

Gwen caught Matty's quiet assessment. "What?"

"You really *are* attracted to him, aren't you?"

Gwen straightened her shoulders and cleared her throat. "Physical attraction can trap you into bad relationships," she said as if reciting a line from a book.

"It can." Butch had proven that theory to Matty, but she was struggling to maintain her optimism about a different outcome with Sebastian. "But just because you're physically attracted to someone doesn't mean the relationship is a mistake."

"It does if you're talking about Travis, which I'd rather not. This reconnaissance mission is supposed to be about you and Sebastian. Let's go."

"Okay." As Matty looked at the peeled-log ranch house with smoke curling from the rock chimney, longing gripped her. If only this could be her home, and the man inside her own true love. "Let's go."

"I'VE HAD easier times with a greased pig!" Travis complained as he started to lower a wiggling and naked Elizabeth into the baby bathtub sitting on the kitchen counter.

"Get your hand under her armpit," Sebastian muttered. "Not like that! Like this." He moved in closer, covered Travis's hand with his and repositioned the wrangler's grip.

Travis turned his head and grinned. "Why, Sebastian, I didn't know you cared."

"Shut up. Jesus! When was the last time you clipped your nails?"

"You didn't tell me I needed a damned manicure for this job."

"If you scratch that baby's skin I'll personally give you a manicure with a hoof knife, cowboy."

"I won't scratch her, okay? If you're gonna be so

damned worried about it, maybe you should give her a bath."

"Nope. You're doing it, and I'm watching. Here's the washcloth. Get her hair wet so we can work the shampoo in."

Elizabeth stared up at Travis and Sebastian. As Travis rubbed the washcloth over her hair she began kicking her feet.

"Whoa, Lizzie!" Travis dropped the washcloth in the water and grabbed both her feet in one large hand. The baby gurgled at him and stopped kicking.

"She'll do that from time to time," Sebastian said with some pride. "Doesn't hurt anything."

"You could've warned me. I thought she was having some sort of fit."

Sebastian snorted. This was one dumb cowboy when it came to babies. "Here's the shampoo. Just a little drop of it's enough."

Travis starting working the shampoo in. "There's something wrong with her hair."

"Like what?"

"It's the same color as mine, but it's not as thick as mine. I always had thick hair."

"See? It's not the Evans' hair!"

"Sure it is. Just thin. Maybe she has a condition. Have you had her checked?"

"There is nothing wrong with her damned hair, Travis. For God's sake."

"I think we should have it checked. Hair's important." As Travis started rinsing the shampoo out, Elizabeth twisted in his grip and started to squall.

"What did you do to her?" Sebastian crowded in next to Travis. "I'll bet you got soap in her eyes."

"Did not. Now move the hell over. You're in my way."

"You pinched her or something. She doesn't cry for no reason." Sebastian held his position and leaned over the baby. "What's the matter, sweetheart? Want your rubber ducky? I'll bet that's it. I forgot your rubber ducky, didn't I, Elizabeth?"

"Can you believe this guy, Lizzie? He starts me out with a handicap, a duckless bath, so he can look like some certified baby expert."

"That's how it is with some people, Elizabeth. They blame you for their own insecurities."

"Bite me, Sebastian."

"Watch how you talk in front of her!"

The doorbell chimed.

"I'll get that," Sebastian said. "Don't do anything until I get back." Every time the doorbell rang, he imagined Jessica standing on the porch. At this point he *really* wanted some answers.

"Get the duck first," Travis said.

"Yeah, okay. I guess you can play with the duck." He found the yellow rubber ducky in the bathroom, walked back and tossed it to Travis, who immediately started squeaking the thing and zooming it through the air like a jet fighter.

"Be careful with her."

"Okay, Mother Sebastian, I'll be *so* careful."

Sebastian scowled at him.

Travis chuckled. "Lighten up, buddy. You'll turn this kid into a pruneface if you keep up that attitude, right, Lizzie?" He looked cross-eyed at the baby.

With Elizabeth's traitorous laughter ringing in his ears, Sebastian headed for the front door. When he glanced out the window and recognized Gwen's violet truck, his heart rate slowed. No Jessica.

Then he opened the door and saw Matty standing there with Gwen, and his pulse skyrocketed again. He should have called her. He really should have called her.

God, she was beautiful. She was wearing her hair down again today, something she seemed to be doing more lately. His hungry gaze took in her crisp jeans, bright red shirt and denim jacket. Then he mentally divested her of all those clothes.

"What's Travis doing here?" Matty asked.

Sebastian snapped out of his trance and realized he'd left them standing there without inviting them in while he daydreamed about making love to Matty. And she'd just asked the million-dollar question. When she got her answer she'd probably be ticked that he hadn't let her know last night. He wasn't sure what to say, especially with Gwen standing there. He wasn't about to pour out his heart in front of an audience.

"Uh, come on in." He opened the door wider and stepped back. "Travis, he—"

Travis's deep laughter rolled out of the kitchen, followed by baby giggles and sharp squeaks from the duck.

Both women's eyes widened.

"Bath time," Sebastian said.

Gwen looked startled. "He's giving that baby a bath?"

"Yeah." For the first time he noticed she was carrying a real pretty blanket, one she'd probably made for Elizabeth. He shifted uneasily as the cheerful noise from the kitchen escalated. "It's Travis's first time at this, so I need to go check on him. You're welcome to come along."

"I wouldn't miss this for the world." Matty started toward the kitchen.

"Me, either." Gwen dropped the blanket across the back of the rocker before following Matty.

Sebastian thought the blanket looked perfect there. In fact, he was enjoying this house much more now that baby stuff was scattered everywhere. "Is that for Elizabeth?"

"Oh. Yeah." Gwen didn't seem much interested in the blanket. All her attention was focused on the kitchen.

"That's great," Sebastian said. "Thanks, Gwen."

"Sure," she said over her shoulder.

As Sebastian followed her into the kitchen he realized that he hadn't told Travis to keep quiet about Jessica and whatever trouble she might be in. But his worry about that vanished in the face of a more immediate worry. Against Sebastian's orders, Travis had taken Elizabeth *out of the tub,* wrapped her in a towel and was buzzing *her* around the room like a jet fighter.

Matty and Gwen stood watching, their mouths open. Travis obviously hadn't seen them yet, and Elizabeth seemed to be having a wonderful time.

Lucky for Travis he wasn't being rough, and he kept Elizabeth in close to his body. He was buzzing her around the room more like an old prop-plane, not like a jet, so he'd get to live. But he was skating on thin ice.

Sebastian moved in. "I'll take her now," he said briskly.

Travis turned, his lips still vibrating from the engine noise he was imitating. He froze in place when he saw Gwen and Matty standing in the kitchen doorway. Slowly he straightened and cradled Elizabeth against his chest as a flush moved up from the collar of his pearl-buttoned western shirt. "Hey," he said weakly. "What's up, ladies?"

Matty spoke first. "I didn't know you were back in Colorado."

"Just got here last night." He glanced down at Elizabeth, then over at Matty and Gwen. "This is sort of embarrassing, but I think...uh, it looks like...this little girl might be—"

"Mine," Sebastian hurried to say.

"Mine," Travis echoed, glaring at Sebastian. "Jessica named me a godfather, same as you, and there's a better chance that I—"

"She delivered the baby to me," Sebastian said. "What does that tell you?"

"That she knew where you lived, bro!"

"Hold it." Gwen couldn't seem to take her gaze from Travis holding that baby. "Isn't Jessica the woman who was in the avalanche with all you guys two years ago?"

"Yeah," Travis said, "and—"

"I'm not sure we should go into it," Sebastian said. He didn't dare look at Matty. He could feel her tension from across the room. He should have called. Even if he still didn't know exactly what to do. Even if he still thought Elizabeth had his eyes.

Matty sighed heavily, and there was a world of meaning in that sigh. "I vote you go into it. You both know you can trust Gwen, and I...deserve to know what was in that second letter."

"Yeah, you do." He glanced at her and winced at

the pain of betrayal in those blue eyes. Damn. "I should have called you last night, Matty."

Her chin came up. "Not necessarily. I don't have a leash on you, Sebastian."

He'd hurt her, and he felt like horse crap. "I know, but—"

"This isn't the place," she said. "Travis, would you like to tell us what was in your letter?"

"I'd be glad to, but first maybe we'd better get Lizzie dressed."

"I'll do it," Sebastian said, wanting an escape from Matty's gaze. "You can get these women some coffee and tell them what's been going on."

"I can dress her," Travis said.

"No, you can't. You don't know where anything is. You've only been through the undressing phase."

Travis winked at Gwen. "Yeah, well, I always was better at that part."

Sebastian shook his head. Leave it to Evans to turn any situation, no matter how awkward, into an opportunity to flirt. People skills came second nature to him, while Sebastian had just managed to alienate the best friend he had in the world.

15

MATTY TRIED TO NUMB her feelings as Travis gave them coffee and led the way into the living room.

"Have a seat." He took a position on the sofa. "Now, I gather from what Sebastian said that Matty knows some of this."

"Some." Matty walked over to the fireplace, where the fire had almost died out. The men had been too busy to keep it built up this morning. She knew from first-hand experience how much time Elizabeth demanded, but surely Sebastian could have found five minutes to call her.

Gwen claimed the wing chair, probably to avoid sitting on the sofa with Travis. "I know nothing except that about three weeks ago a baby appeared at the Rocking D. I found out when I met Sebastian and Matty buying baby furniture at Coogan's."

Matty sent her a grateful glance. Gwen wasn't the type to blurt out that Matty had stayed overnight here, much less that Matty and Sebastian had made love, but Gwen was distracted and nervous. Matty appreciated the fact that she'd kept her head and not betrayed any confidences.

Travis glanced at Matty. "You can sit down, too, Matty. You make me nervous prowling back and forth in front of the fireplace."

The problem was that she didn't know where to

sit. The room was filled with bittersweet memories, memories she hoped to quickly get away from once she learned the information Sebastian hadn't seen fit to tell her. If he'd felt as connected to her as she did to him, he would have called her within minutes of finding out that Jessica had also named Travis as a godfather.

Obviously Sebastian had been caught up in the moment three weeks ago. So much for his claim that he wanted her desperately and had only sent her away because he had an obligation to keep himself free for Jessica. When that obligation became blurred, Sebastian hadn't said a word to Matty. And that spoke volumes.

She finally chose to sit next to Travis on the sofa because the other choice was the rocker. She couldn't risk reliving the warmth of rocking the baby with Sebastian hovering nearby and a snowstorm creating a delicious sense of intimacy.

Taking a sip of her coffee, she directed her explanation to Gwen. "Elizabeth's mother is Jessica, the woman who was skiing with the guys when that avalanche took place in Aspen two years ago on Sebastian's birthday."

"I see," Gwen said. "Didn't you guys go back up there last year for another celebration?"

Matty gave her friend credit for sounded vaguely unsure about the information. Gwen knew all about them going skiing again, because Matty had cried on Gwen's shoulder when Sebastian hadn't stayed home for his birthday, thus depriving Matty of a chance to have a little party for him.

Travis nodded. "Yep, we went back last year. All

except Nat, who had some conflict and couldn't make it."

Gwen gazed at him. "That was almost twelve months ago. And now both of you are claiming to be the father of this three-month-old baby." She shook her head. "Forgive me, but that conjures up a scenario I don't even want to think about."

"Hey," Travis said. "Give us some credit. We might not know exactly what happened, but we sure as hell didn't have an orgy going on. Jessica's not the type and neither are we."

"You're going to have a hard time convincing people of that if you both keep claiming to be Elizabeth's father."

Travis hunkered forward and lowered his voice. "I'm sure it's me. I'm not proud of admitting I was the one, but you can't tell me Sebastian Daniels would get so drunk that he'd have sex with a woman he didn't love and then not even bother to use protection." He glanced at Matty. "You've known him for longer than any of us. Can you picture that?"

Not trusting herself to speak, Matty shook her head.

"Me, either. Totally out of character. The guy's a rock of discipline and morals. The rest of us have always counted on Sebastian to do the right thing."

Matty's brain was spinning, but one thought kept popping out of the whirlpool, one that would explain everything. "Are you sure he doesn't love her?"

Travis's gaze was steady, and understanding settled into his golden eyes. "I'm sure, Matty," he said quietly. "He doesn't talk about her the way a man talks about a woman he loves. Besides, think about it. If Sebastian loved Jessica, he'd be tearing around looking for her, no matter what she said in the note."

"I guess so." Matty tried to sound casual, but she was afraid from the expression on Travis's face that he had just figured out how she felt about Sebastian. "It was just a thought, to help explain things," she added.

"Well, he doesn't love her. In fact—" He hesitated, as if trying to decide whether to say what was on his mind. "In fact, I'm sure of it," he finished, "and I'm also sure he's not Lizzie's father. As for me, it's highly likely. I have a reputation for...well, enjoying myself with the ladies. So even though I can't remember exactly what happened, I'm sure I was the one, even if Jessica's note doesn't name me as the father."

"Now *that* I would believe," Gwen said.

Travis shot her a look of irritation. "On the other hand, even though I've had my share of good times, this is the first baby I've ever been responsible for, which is a damn fine record, in my opinion."

"I'm sure you're a legend in your own time," Gwen said.

"What..." Matty paused and cleared her throat. "What do you plan to do?" She had a wild image of Travis and Sebastian fighting over who would marry Jessica, assuming she'd have either of them.

Travis turned his coffee mug in his work-roughened hands. "Damned if I know. I'd make one lousy husband, so I'd hesitate to ask Jess to marry me, which she probably wouldn't want to do. She'd get a bad deal."

"It's a wise man who knows himself," Gwen said.

Travis glared at her. "Lady, you've got one hell of

a burr under your saddle. You shouldn't let one man sour you on the lot of them."

"I haven't. You and Derek happen to be...similar."

"If you mean we both put our pants on one leg at a time, then you'd be right. Past that, I have nothing in common with your ex."

"That's a matter of—"

"Whoa." Sebastian came into the room with Elizabeth cuddled against his shoulder. "Time out, you two."

Instantly Matty couldn't see anything in the room but Sebastian and Elizabeth. He'd dressed her in a pink terry sleeper with lace on the collar and cuffs. Matty recognized the pink suit. She'd gone with Sebastian to buy some spare outfits, and they'd argued about this one, which Sebastian had wanted and Matty had said was too froufrou for a no-nonsense girl like Elizabeth.

They'd laughed and teased each other during the argument, as if looking for an excuse to enjoy each other's quirks. Matty had watched happily married couples argue in that same way. Seeing the outfit now, Matty felt as if she'd been sucker punched.

Suddenly she wanted to get the hell out of the house. She knew as much as she needed to know. Travis was a more likely candidate to be Elizabeth's father than Sebastian, but for some reason Sebastian didn't want to consider the possibility. As long as he stubbornly believed himself to be the baby's father, he would hold out for marriage and family with Jessica. Whatever he felt for Matty wasn't powerful enough to challenge that drive.

Putting her coffee mug on the lamp table, she

stood. "Obviously you two guys have lots to work out, so maybe we should run along, Gwen."

Gwen put her mug down immediately. "Fine by me. I think Travis would be more comfortable if I left."

Travis pushed himself away from the sofa with such force that he almost spilled his coffee. "Hold on a minute. I have no problem with *you*. You're the one who can't seem to deal with the likes of *me*."

"Well, you have a point, there," Gwen said breezily. She walked around the sofa and tickled Elizabeth's cheek. "Bye, bye, honey lamb." Then she glanced at Sebastian. "I won't say a word to anyone in town, but I think you and studman there had better get your story straight before you go public with it. Multiple fathers only occur in litters of kittens."

Matty wished she could think of a similar snappy exit line, but her heart ached too much for her to think straight. "I'll see you both around," she said. "Whenever you want to stash your stuff, Travis, come on over. We'll be getting the cattle May fifteenth."

"Yeah." Travis gave her a reassuring smile. "I'm sure we'll have this situation worked out by then. Right, Sebastian?"

"Uh, right. See you, Gwen. See you, Matty."

Matty couldn't help herself. She had to allow herself one last look at him and that beautiful baby. She met his troubled gaze and her heart ached with regret. "See you, Sebastian and Elizabeth."

"YOU IDIOT!" Travis whirled toward Sebastian the minute the door closed after Matty and Gwen. "That woman's in love with you!"

"I know," Sebastian said quietly.

"And unless I miss my guess, you feel the same about her."

Sebastian nodded. He felt as if somebody had shoved him into a snowbank and left him there to freeze. "I figure I've been in love with Matty Lang for nearly ten years. I just didn't know it until three weeks ago."

"And now that I think about it, she's been sweet on you for a hell of a long time, too. I just wasn't paying attention before. So how come you're letting her walk out that door with that look of pure misery on her face?"

Elizabeth started to fuss and Sebastian headed toward the kitchen. Damned if he would justify himself to Travis. "The baby needs her bottle."

"Then we'll get her the doggone bottle, but I'm not backing off, Sebastian." Travis followed him into the kitchen. "Matty's not only my boss, she's a fine lady, the best. You're a helluva lucky man, and you don't seem to realize that fact."

"Oh, I realize it." Mechanically Sebastian went through his routine, settling Elizabeth in her infant seat and fastening the straps. She whimpered and twisted in her seat, but he knew she'd quiet down faster if he got her bottle ready instead of entertaining her. "Matty's the unlucky one, setting her sights on me."

"She sure is, if this is the way you treat her."

"How can I encourage her? If I'm Elizabeth's father, then...then I should probably marry Jessica." But he didn't know how he could make himself do that anymore, even if it was the honorable thing.

"Oh, *that* makes sense."

"Maybe not to you, but it's the only way I know to handle this."

"You poor misguided sap."

Muttering an oath, Sebastian turned away from him.

"And, off the subject a little, what's with the tie-downs here on the kid?" Travis asked. "She obviously hates it."

Sebastian shrugged. He felt dead inside, numb with grief because he'd hurt Matty, the last person on earth he ever wanted to hurt. "I have to put her somewhere safe while I fix her bottle."

"The hell with that." Travis unhooked the strap and picked up the baby. "Hey, Lizzie, girl! Can I have this dance? You'd be delighted? That's how I like my women. Delighted." He started two-stepping around the kitchen while he hummed a Reba McEntire tune.

Sebastian finished fixing the bottle and turned toward Travis. "Okay, Fred Astaire. I'm ready."

Travis had switched to a waltz and had his cheek pressed to Elizabeth's as he spun her in graceful circles. "Me and Lizzie have a good thing going. Let us finish this song."

Sebastian battled free-floating anger that was searching for a target. He let it settle on Travis and his devil-may-care attitude. "Move it, Travis. I don't have time to stand around here waiting for you to finish the damned song."

Travis whirled to a stop and fixed his gaze on Sebastian. "How does it feel to be a martyr? Are you enjoying making everybody miserable, Dudley Do-Right?"

Anger boiled in him now, hot and strong as campfire coffee. "So help me, God, if you weren't holding that baby..."

"But I am. And while Lizzie's protecting me from having my jaw broken, I'll tell you that I'd take a hundred-to-one odds that you're not this kid's daddy. But even if you are, you and Jess don't belong together. You might be willing to sacrifice yourself to the cause, but I give her credit for more sense."

Sebastian clenched the bottle in a death grip. "She'd want to do the best thing for Elizabeth."

"And that would be marrying you and settling down at the Rocking D?"

Sebastian opened his mouth to reply and realized he hadn't thought that through yet, either.

"Because I know you, Sebastian, and you're planted here as sure as those aspens you stuck in the ground out front. Jessica's not a ranch woman, and you damn well know it."

"She might learn to like it," Sebastian insisted, although he no longer believed that. He had been a misguided sap, like Travis said.

"Oh, that's another good idea. Like Barbara learned?"

"Okay, then I'll—"

"Don't even tell me you'll sell the ranch. Nat's been trying to get you to do that for years, every time he finds another wealthy client, and we all know it'll never happen. Might as well cut your heart out with a hacksaw. So we have Jess who isn't a ranch woman, and we have Matty, who is, and she'll be living down the road from you, same as always, because she's as planted here as you are."

Sebastian knew that. Matty had always said she wanted to be buried in her backyard.

"Don't you think that Jess would eventually figure out you're in love with the neighbor? And loving Matty and not doing anything about it makes you one son of a bitch to live with. I can testify to that after less than twenty-four hours! What a wonderful atmosphere you'd create for this kid."

Sebastian couldn't think straight anymore. At first he'd known exactly what to do. Yet recently he'd figured out his plans were full of holes. He couldn't marry Jessica when he was in love with Matty. He couldn't expect Jessica to marry him and live on this ranch. They'd have to work out something else, some sort of joint custody. He knew all that, but he was furious with Travis for pointing out what an idiot he'd been. "I'd like to know what makes you such an expert on raising kids!"

"I'm not. But I know women. And I know Matty. She feels things real deep. If you don't fix this situation pretty damned quick, it'll be permanently broke. And if that happens you stand a real good chance of ending up alone, cowboy."

MATTY AND Gwen drove to the Leaning L in silence. Matty didn't want to talk and she figured Gwen was stumped for what to say. There was nothing to say. Matty had been bushwacked. Again.

As Gwen pulled up in front of the house, she glanced over at Matty. "Are you all right?"

Matty didn't think she'd ever be all right again. But she was sick to death of being poor little Matty, who always got the rough end of the stick. She took a deep breath and turned to Gwen. "How long's it been since you've been honky-tonkin'?"

GWEN HAD LEAPED at the suggestion, although Matty figured Gwen would have leaped at the idea of hang gliding if she thought it would help Matty get through her heartbreak. She insisted Matty grab her party clothes and bring them to Hawthorne House so they could get dressed together and Gwen could give Matty a makeover.

And that was how Matty ended up getting the attention of every unattached guy hanging out at the bar when she walked into the Buckskin with Gwen that night. As she slipped out of her coat, eyes widened and jaws dropped. She'd never made such a stir in her life, and it felt damned good.

She hadn't been here since Butch died, but the place hadn't changed. The band might be different, but the rhythm of the tunes and the twang of electric guitars sounded achingly familiar, reminding her of outings with Barbara, Butch...and Sebastian. Same scuffed dance floor, same neon signs, same cluster of tables with red-glass hurricane lamps, same scent of beer and peanuts.

"I think you're a hit," Gwen murmured as they found a table near the dance floor. "They're still scraping their tongues off the floor."

"It's the shock of discovering that I have legs." Matty was thrilled that the outfit was a success, but she was a little self-conscious, too. "I still can't believe you chopped off my best dancing skirt. It barely covers the essentials."

"That's the whole idea. They may spend so much

time ogling your legs, they'll miss my inspired job on your makeup."

"I think the makeup's overdone."

"Matty, you think anything besides lipstick is overdone. Trust me, you look great."

"Well, my hair feels weird. Like there's too much of it."

"It looks fantastic, too." Gwen cocked her head to admire Matty's curls. "I'm going to teach you how to use the curling iron, so you can do the same thing yourself. Hair like yours needs to bounce and create some excitement."

Matty rolled her eyes and grinned. "You've been itching to fix me for years, haven't you?"

"Yes, as a matter of fact, I have."

Matty gazed at her friend. "Thanks, Gwen. For taking my mind off...well, you know."

"I know." Her glance flicked toward a couple of cowboys approaching the table. "And now I think someone else is ready to take over the job."

Matty tensed. Playing dress-up had been fun, more fun than she would have expected. She'd welcomed the ego boost of having men stare at her with obvious admiration. But now came the real test—to see if she could tolerate another man besides Sebastian touching her. But she'd come here to have a good time, and she wasn't about to back down now.

She turned toward the two men and noticed one of them was Cyrus from the feed store. Dredging up all her willpower, she gave him a brilliant smile of welcome. Time to get on with her life.

SEBASTIAN FELT as if he'd lost an arm when he left the house without Elizabeth. He hadn't been more than twenty feet away from the baby since she'd arrived, except for the short time he'd spent picking up Matty's stuff that first night. He'd waited until after Elizabeth had drifted off to sleep before he left, and he hoped to God Travis didn't do something stupid while he was gone.

It had taken him a half hour to leave. He'd armed Travis with two more bottles, Jessica's written instructions and another page of his own notes. He'd made sure there were plenty of diapers and clean outfits, and Travis had promised to spend the evening reading the baby book.

Still Sebastian had to force himself to climb in the truck and drive away. He'd never much liked cell phones, but he wished he had one now. All the way over to Matty's, he envisioned disaster. Travis might mean well, but he didn't have enough experience to be put in charge of Elizabeth.

But there was no alternative. Sebastian had to put Matty first this time, and he needed to talk to her with no distractions. What he had to say would be difficult enough without having to take care of Elizabeth while he was saying it.

He hated being wrong, but he'd been wrong. After Travis had finished saying his piece, Sebastian had sat in the rocker feeding Elizabeth and thinking about how he could make it up to Matty for hurting her.

His plan to marry Jessica had been stupid, and insisting on it had shoved a knife through Matty's heart. He still longed for the assurance that he'd see Elizabeth every day as she grew up, but that wasn't realistic. The price, denying his love for Matty and trying to make a life with Jessica, was too high. Everyone would suffer, including Elizabeth.

So he was going to see Matty, and he only hoped he wasn't too late.

Her truck was in the drive, and his heart pounded in anticipation as he rang the doorbell. He rehearsed what he would say, what he would do. He pictured her inside, brokenhearted and blue, all because of him. But on the second ring, as Sadie barked on the other side of the door, he knew Matty wasn't home.

Damn. She was with Gwen—he'd bet money on it. No doubt she was crying her little heart out on Gwen's sympathetic shoulder, and he didn't blame her for that. He didn't relish saying his piece in front of Gwen. Yet he didn't want to go home without seeing Matty, either. He headed for town.

In his concentration, he almost missed the violet truck parked outside the Buckskin as he sped past. Then he nearly caused an accident when he swerved the Bronco in a sharp U-turn and barreled back to the night spot.

So the girls had stopped in for a beer, he thought. Understandable. He pictured them huddled at a back table, Gwen handing tissues to Matty. He was lower than a snake's belly to make her cry like that. Once he was inside the bar he'd wait for a slow dance, get her out on the floor and tell her how sorry he was, how he'd spend a lifetime making it up to her.

He parked the truck and walked toward the building. Yeah, a slow dance would be perfect. As he pushed through the swinging door, he pictured the scene. He'd kiss the tears away, and promise her the world. He'd—

Do nothing of the kind.

First of all, Matty was not in some dark corner. She was cavorting in the middle of a stomping, clapping circle of cowboys and cowgirls with...Cyrus! Worse yet, she was wearing a *skirt!* Or some people might call it that. Sebastian called it indecent exposure, especially when Cyrus twirled her. And her hair was all curly and bouncing around, and her lips were bright red. She looked—Sebastian groaned—sexy as hell.

And worst of all, she was *smiling.* Smiling at that wet-behind-the-ears cowpoke who wasn't fit to wipe her boots.

Instinct took over as he pushed through the crowd and grabbed hold of Matty's arm. Cyrus put up some resistance when Sebastian hauled Matty away, but the look in Sebastian's eyes must have scared him some, because he backed off.

Matty was a different story. She kicked him so hard in his kneecap that he wondered if she broke it. The band stopped playing and everybody stared.

"How dare you?" she cried, trying to pull away from him.

"Would you come outside for a minute?" he asked hopefully.

"No, I will not! You can say what you have to say right here!"

He winced. Nothing in the world was harder for him than airing his dirty laundry in public. He'd hoped not to have the whole damn valley know his business this time around. But Matty was madder than he'd ever seen her. She looked like she was getting ready to kick him again, and this time she might aim for something besides his kneecap.

"You turn me loose, Sebastian Daniels," she hissed, "or I'll do some real damage."

He swallowed and tried to forget the throbbing in his knee. It looked like he had a choice. He could either bare his soul for the entire crowd gathered in the dance hall, or he could forget about winning Matty.

It was no contest. "I love you, Matty," he said, thinking that might mellow her some and convince her to come outside with him for the rest of his speech.

It didn't work. She twisted more vigorously in her attempt to get away from him. "So what? I love you, too, but you aren't planning to do anything about it, so why waste your breath telling me?"

He'd have to do the whole number right now, in front of the world. "Because I think we should get married."

She stilled for a moment, and some of the rage left her blue eyes. But then it came roaring back and she struggled against him with new energy. "Oh, I get it. Jessica called, didn't she? Well, I don't care to be second choice, cowboy. So take your marriage proposal and put it where the sun don't shine!"

"Jessica didn't call. I just figured out that..." Oh, boy. Talk about public humiliation. The heat of a flush crept up from his shirt collar as the room went dead silent. He felt all those eyes trained right on him.

But his future with Matty was at stake. "I figured out that I was wrong about...everything. I've loved you for years, Matty, without realizing it, and we've wasted too much time already. So I'd appreciate it if you'd—"

She nearly knocked the breath from him when she

launched herself into his arms. Staggering backward, he managed to keep them both upright as he looked into eyes bright with love and damp with tears. And slowly their audience faded as he became totally mesmerized by Matty's beloved face.

"For years?" she whispered in a voice choked with emotion.

"And years," he murmured. "Will you marry me, Matty Lang?" And he waited, heart pounding, for the most important words of his life.

She gazed up at him and blinked back the tears. "Yes, Sebastian Daniels, I will." Then the tears rolled unchecked down her cheeks as he kissed her.

Which cowboy should baby Elizabeth call Daddy? Sebastian? Travis? Or somebody altogether different? The mystery continues in TWO IN THE SADDLE, Book Two in the THREE COWBOYS & A BABY mini-series, available next month.

HARLEQUIN® Temptation.

Cowboys.
Every boy's hero...every woman's fantasy.
They can rope, they can ride...
But can they change a diaper?

What happens when three intrepid cowpokes bravely go
where none of them had ever *dreamed* of going before—
the nursery!

Find out in **Vicki Lewis Thompson**'s
wonderful new miniseries...

THREE COWBOYS AND A BABY

Temptation #780 *THE COLORADO KID*, April 2000
Temptation #784 *TWO IN THE SADDLE*, May 2000
Temptation #788 *BOONE'S BOUNTY*, June 2000
and
Harlequin Single Title, *THAT'S MY BABY!*,
September 2000

Don't miss these tender, sexy love stories,
written by one of Harlequin's most beloved authors.

Available wherever Harlequin books are sold.

HARLEQUIN®
Makes any time special ™

Visit us at www.romance.net

HT3COW

If you enjoyed what you just read,
then we've got an offer you can't resist!

Take 2 bestselling
love stories FREE!
Plus get a FREE surprise gift!

Clip this page and mail it to Harlequin Reader Service®

IN U.S.A.	IN CANADA
3010 Walden Ave.	P.O. Box 609
P.O. Box 1867	Fort Erie, Ontario
Buffalo, N.Y. 14240-1867	L2A 5X3

YES! Please send me 2 free Harlequin Temptation® novels and my free surprise gift. Then send me 4 brand-new novels every month, which I will receive before they're available in stores. In the U.S.A., bill me at the bargain price of $3.34 plus 25¢ delivery per book and applicable sales tax, if any*. In Canada, bill me at the bargain price of $3.80 plus 25¢ delivery per book and applicable taxes**. That's the complete price and a savings of 10% off the cover prices—what a great deal! I understand that accepting the 2 free books and gift places me under no obligation ever to buy any books. I can always return a shipment and cancel at any time. Even if I never buy another book from Harlequin, the 2 free books and gift are mine to keep forever. So why not take us up on our invitation. You'll be glad you did!

142 HEN C22U

342 HEN C22V

Name	(PLEASE PRINT)	
Address	Apt.#	
City	State/Prov.	Zip/Postal Code

* Terms and prices subject to change without notice. Sales tax applicable in N.Y.
** Canadian residents will be charged applicable provincial taxes and GST.
 All orders subject to approval. Offer limited to one per household.
 ® are registered trademarks of Harlequin Enterprises Limited.

TEMP00   ©1998 Harlequin Enterprises Limited

Back by popular demand are

DEBBIE MACOMBER's

Hard Luck, Alaska, is a
town that needs women!
And the O'Halloran brothers
are just the fellows
to fly them in.

Starting in March 2000 this beloved series returns
in special 2-in-1 collector's editions:

MAIL-ORDER MARRIAGES, featuring
Brides for Brothers and *The Marriage Risk*
On sale March 2000

FAMILY MEN, featuring
Daddy's Little Helper and *Because of the Baby*
On sale July 2000

THE LAST TWO BACHELORS, featuring
Falling for Him and *Ending in Marriage*
On sale August 2000

Collect and enjoy each MIDNIGHT SONS story!

Available at your favorite retail outlet.

HARLEQUIN®
Makes any time special ™

Visit us at www.romance.net

PHMS

ATTENTION ALL ROMANCE READERS—

There's an
incredible offer
waiting for you!

For a limited time only, Harlequin will mail you
your **Free Guide** to the World of Romance

inside
romance

Get to know your **Favorite Authors,** such as
Diana Palmer and **Nora Roberts**
through in-depth biographies

Be the first to know about **New Titles**

Read Highlights from your
Favorite Romance Series

And take advantage of
Special Offers and **Contests**

Act now by visiting us online at

www.eHarlequin.com/rtlnewsletter

**Where all your romance news
is waiting for you!**

PNEWS

HEART OF THE WEST

Every Man Has His Price!

Lost Springs Ranch was
famous for turning young
mavericks into good men.
So word that the ranch was
in financial trouble sent
a herd of loyal bachelors
stampeding back to
Wyoming to put themselves
on the auction block!

July 1999	*Husband for Hire* Susan Wiggs	January 2000	*The Rancher and the Rich Girl* Heather MacAllister
August	*Courting Callie* Lynn Erickson	February	*Shane's Last Stand* Ruth Jean Dale
September	*Bachelor Father* Vicki Lewis Thompson	March	*A Baby by Chance* Cathy Gillen Thacker
October	*His Bodyguard* Muriel Jensen	April	*The Perfect Solution* Day Leclaire
November	*It Takes a Cowboy* Gina Wilkins	May	*Rent-a-Dad* Judy Christenberry
December	*Hitched by Christmas* Jule McBride	June	*Best Man in Wyoming* Margot Dalton

HARLEQUIN®
Makes any time special ™

Visit us at www.romance.net

PHHOWGEN